QUIESCENT: BLOOD FEUD
UNCOVERED DARKNESS SERIES: BOOK 3

ASHON RUFFINS

Copyright © 2025 by Ashon Ruffins and Dreadful Times Press, LLC

All rights reserved.

No part of this book may be reproduced in any form or by any electronic or mechanical means, including information storage and retrieval systems, without written permission from the author, except for the use of brief quotations in a book review.

All associated logos are trademarks and/or registered trademarks of Dreadful Times Press, LLC.

Edited by : Stand Corrected Editing

Poisoned Ink Press

Cover Design by: Fay Lane Graphic Design

ISBN: 979-8-9855902-6-5

To K.A.T.
Thank you for the thrilling ride

QUIESCENT: BLOOD FEUD

(Uncovered Darkness Series: Book 3)

By Ashon Ruffins

PROLOGUE

It wasn't the darkness that bothered me. It was the damned smell. The city had its own distinct odor, but the dank and earthy aroma of the swamp was unparalleled. The best part about a stakeout was the snacks. Not tonight. That sour stench was potent enough to destroy an appetite. I didn't get the dopamine rush from the chocolate I brought with me. Putting down this cryptid would be a better adrenaline rush. Something had to pay off the late hours of gazing into the pitch-black void littered with moss-covered trees and swamp water. A cabin that appeared to be a century old, decayed and molded, precariously rested near the tree line. The structure had to be deserted because its shattered windows and fractured roof wouldn't be optimal living conditions for a human, even one that would favor the swamp. The ring of the cell phone on the seat beside me was a welcomed distraction. Moreso, the name displayed on the illuminated screen caused me to smile as I answered.

"Tammy, perfect timing. I was terribly nauseated and bored," I said.

A timid giggle on the other end of the line followed. "Hey, Nola. Good to hear your voice. What are you doing that's so monotonous? It's not exactly how I would describe your life."

"Girl, I'm scoping out this swamp area and it's been dead for hours. On top of it all, it stinks out here! You know how smells get to me. This is killing my snack cravings."

"Oh, that sucks. What are you hunting that has you staking out a swamp?" Tammy asked.

I snatched the binoculars from my lap and peered through them as I placed the call on speakerphone. Only the front of the obscure tree line was apparent from where I sat, and it was just as still as it was hours before.

"Something old that was rumored to have been seen in this area. A cryptid the locals called The Grunch. Based on everything I've learned, it's an especially vicious creature," I said.

"The Grunch? That name makes it sound dreadful," Tammy said.

"Well, this thing is believed to be approximately two hundred years old and is rumored to be half man, half beast with horns like a goat. It also loves the taste of blood, both human and animal. So, yeah. Pretty horrible," I said.

"Sounds to me like you should have the team with you," Tammy replied.

"I'm not technically on a hunt. Just a scout to see what I might be dealing with. That's if I can find the damned thing. Based on everything I've read and all chatter with some of the folks that live in the area, not many people have put their eyes on it. This creature has done an adequate job of persisting in the shadows."

"Nola, just do me a favor and watch your ass. Jackson can't afford to lose you."

"Speaking of that little troublemaker, Jackson was the reason I asked you to call me. Will you still make it here for his birthday? I would love to surprise him," I said.

"I wouldn't miss it for the world. I just spoke with him a couple of days ago. Jackson seems to be doing well, and he didn't mention anything about an upcoming party. So, I think the cat is still in the bag." Tammy followed with a little snort of amusement. "Where is Jackson anyway? He could have kept you company on the stakeout."

"Jackson said he and Chloe had plans. I get it. He's a young college man in love. Of course, he has plans with his girlfriend."

"Those two really bonded, didn't they?" Tammy said.

The notion of Jackson and the newly formed motherly instincts piqued my curiosity. I picked up my cell phone and confirmed Jackson's whereabouts. The tiny pin on the screen caused me to huff in confusion.

"Wait. Why is he in a grav—,"

The snap of the rustling tree line and the bright yellow burn of what looked like two eyes emerging from the obscurity of the blackness captivated my attention.

"Tammy, let me call you back," I said, hanging up the phone and peering through the binoculars as I leaned forward over the steering wheel.

With eyes stretched wide, I watched as a creature emerged from the darkness, filling the sight field of the binoculars. My mouth opened at the sight of it. Its slow hoofed track under the moonlight allowed for a clear visual of the creature's horrific features. The urban legends were exactly right in its depictions. The Grunch was easily over six feet in height, with massive ram horns adorned on both sides of its head and a nasty set of jagged teeth as an accessory. Half-man and half-beast, the full display of its powerful frame trekked toward the dilapidated, stilted wooded structure. Its legs sloshed through the swamp water effortlessly as it carried what appeared to be the pale naked corpse of a woman over its shoulder. Circular bite marks, soaked in blood, covered her back.

"Well, shit. I guess I shouldn't be surprised this thing actually exists. Four painstaking days parked on the edge of this swamp, every evening, and finally this thing showed itself, in all its horrific glory."

Stories of its ferocity and the gruesomeness of its appearance sometimes convoluted tales told by locals. That wasn't the case this time. Every physical detail and behavioral pattern provided by surrounding townspeople was spot on, except for one. No one knew how to kill this thing. From everything I've gathered, this creature dated back hundreds of years, and there hadn't been one text or word from someone familiar with this monstrosity that could provide any information on how to injure or kill it.

The Grunch made its way to the cabin and flung the body of the woman onto the aged and decaying wooden porch. The sight of its dense hide and animal-like movement resulted in short breaths as my chest constricted.

"God, not now. This is not the time for an anxiety attack." I took slower, deeper breaths to help slow the increased pounding in my chest. "Tammy was right. I should have someone with me. I can't chance confronting this thing with only silver. Who knows if silver has any effect on it? Time to go."

I turned the ignition and started the car. The automatic

lights were an unexpected consequence. A slight lapse in judgement while I focused to get my breathing under control. The Grunch turned toward the brightness of the headlights of the car. Its spiked teeth and disfigured face were clear as daylight. It relayed a twisted grin in silence upon its discovery of me. I pulled the gear into reverse and slammed the gas pedal.

As I drove away, I darted my eyes at the rear-view mirror and watched the Grunch lower its horned head and charge toward me. The tail end of the car swerved as the tires tried to strengthen their grip on the moistened dirt beneath them. Blood drained from my knuckles as my grip of the steering wheel tightened while the car accelerated down the road. The sight of the Grunch in the rearview mirror grew closer and larger as it gained ground. It rammed the back of the car, lifting it briefly off its rear tires and back to the ground.

My eyes darted in the direction of the side-view mirror as the beast pulled up and stood, watching me drive away. I continued to speed away as I made my way onto the interstate and back toward The Big Easy... New Orleans.

"I'll just keep this miscalculation to myself. No need to worry the boys."

CHAPTER ONE

"ZOMBIES DON'T EXIST. THAT'S JUST HOLLYWOOD BULLSHIT."—JACKSON

Four years after the events in Dalyville.

Saturday—Ten days before Mardi Gras.

On any other day, Jackson had no issues making jokes about the fog that hovered low as he and Chloe arrived at the abandoned graveyard in Algiers. It exuded cheesy horror movie vibes. Jackson never enjoyed taking the fifteen-minute trip to the Westbank of New Orleans. He found it to be cumbersome. The formidable height of the steel bridge that towered in the sky of the Crescent City, and spanned the width of the muddy Mississippi River, Jackson's legs tingled in fear when he drove across it. Images of the narrow lanes and the potential for drowning in his wrecked truck after a crash preoccupied his thoughts. Jackson's hands gripped the steering wheel a little tighter. The drive almost always triggered his anxiety and acrophobia. It was his secret shame. Evil didn't confine itself or take time to avoid the Westbank of New Orleans because of inconvenience. In fact, it was the exact opposite. Evil was without limits. It would go wherever necessary to feast on the flesh and blood of anyone or anything it could sink its teeth into.

The fog was thick enough to cause a bit of concern for Jackson. This hunt was dangerous enough without the need to fight through sight obstructions. After all, he had taken the time to sneak away from his Auntie Nola to take this hunt alone. Well, almost alone. Chloe insisted on tagging along. She sought extensive knowledge of the world's malevolent entities and their eradication after she listened to Jackson's stories. It didn't hurt that Chloe wanted to be by his side every step of the way.

Jackson loved her enthusiasm. Her energy matched his own, and she was one of the few people around who picked up on his sarcastic sense of humor. Still, Jackson had reservations about whether it was the right thing to do to bring her along. He could almost hear Nola in his head lecturing him on the danger, nagging him on the responsibility he had to protect people like Chloe. The innocent, everyday people that only wanted to live their lives without interference. It was one reason that making fun of the trope about the fog in the graveyard was inappropriate. He didn't want to undercut the situation. Jackson was protective of his college sweetheart, and Chloe seemed to be one of the more genuine people he had ever met. What he loved most about her was her edge. The part of her that wanted to embrace the dangers of the hunt.

"Babe, I need you to stay close to me," Jackson said, as he shoved the shift handle of the pickup truck into park after they arrived outside the gate of the cemetery. The pointed arrow tips at the top of the iron rod gate were no longer visible, lost in the depths of the fog. The top of the above ground mausoleum graves inside hid in the thickness.

"I know you've been looking forward to this, but this isn't a game. If what we think is in there is really inside, then we need to be on our A game. Otherwise, we're nothing more than a midnight snack. Do you understand?" Jackson grabbed Chloe's hand. Her knuckles paled as he squeezed.

"I get it, Jackson. Don't worry. I'm not doing this for a thrill. You and your aunt are in the right business, and I want to be a part of it. I had to see it for myself, not just read about it in some internet article," Chloe said as she tied her brownish blonde hair up into a bun above her neck.

"Okay. Okay . . . just stay close. Remember some of the basics I've taught you. If you see me struggling, aim at its head and squeeze the trigger. Don't pull it. Squeeze it and control your breathing," Jackson said as he handed Chloe a black semi-automatic handgun.

With curled lips, he inhaled deeply as he stared back at the grin Chloe had on her face. "Maybe we should rethink this. I'm not sure you're ready. Just stay here in the truck. I'll go in and take care of it. I'll come and get you after."

"Jackson, stop it. I'm more than a big brain and a pretty face. I'm here with you right now. Take advantage of it and stop being condescending," Chloe replied as she quickly hopped down from the truck outside. A small grunt came from her as her feet hit the ground.

Jackson knew Chloe hated his raised pickup truck. She voiced her dismay to him anytime the subject came up. Called it a textbook cliché for a southern guy. Jackson followed as he glared at Chloe through the windows of the truck, eyes widened, and an index finger pressed against his lips. He waved her over to the back of the truck. A large mausoleum was just yards away, so Jackson quietly guided her to crouch behind it for concealment. He stared into Chloe's brown eyes and smiled at her.

"Okay, Miss Bad-Ass," Jackson whispered with a subtle chuckle. "Give me the book report on why we're here."

Chloe playfully punched Jackson on the shoulder. "I am a bad-ass, you jerk." She smiled as she continued. "So, some people have gone missing in this graveyard after reportedly visiting loved ones that passed away. There have also been reports of grave disturbances here in the news, and that's what makes you think it's a girl . . ."

"A ghoul . . ." Jackson corrected, as he lowered his head with a slight chuckle. "I know you said that just to be funny, but this is important. I don't know what or who we'll encounter in there. Anything could have taken those people, and it could be almost anything disturbing those graves. It also could be nothing. But if it's a ghoul, I don't want to end up on its dinner plate. Do you?" The smile on his face vanished as fast as the moon behind the blanketing cover of low-hanging clouds.

Chloe's brow tensed, and her facial expression contorted from playful to terrified in a matter of moments. Not the effect Jackson was going for.

"I get it, baby. So, what's the plan?"

"Same as it was before. Stay close to me. You have the Beretta, but keep it holstered," Jackson said, pointing to Chloe's waist. "It could be anything in there. Vampire. Demon. Probably not a werewolf because Auntie killed all the ones they had in the city. Whatever it is, the first round in that chamber is silver. The others are hollow point. It will be enough for you to slow down whatever it is long enough for you to run back to the truck and get out of here if something happens to me. If it is a ghoul and I'm down for the count, try to hit it in the head a couple of times. That should do it."

"Like a zombie, right?" Chloe responded.

"Zombies don't exist. That's just Hollywood bullshit. Ghouls can be just as ugly, though," Jackson answered. He stood and pulled a thick and long, rubber-grated, black object from his waist. His other hand reached back for Chloe.

Jackson yanked Chloe along, hand in hand, across the wet grass to the ajar mausoleum door. The stone structure must have been impressive years ago. It was easily the size of a cabin or multi-room garage. A prominent life-size, ivory colored stone angel, posed in a kneeling position with its head resting on the handle of a sword. The tip of the blade wedged into the top of the entryway had impressive detailing. Jackson recognized a rich man's burial ground when he saw one. Well, at least eighty or so years ago, it was a rich man. Not so much now.

As he clutched Chloe's hand, Jackson leaned into the heavy stone door and pushed. The weight of the door was unexpected and resisted Jackson's not-so-heavy frame. He didn't have the same muscular build as his father, but he made up for it with his quickness and ingenuity.

Friction from the bottom of the stone door rubbed against the concrete floor and screeched as Jackson managed to push it open a little further. The sound might as well have been a dinner bell ringing as it echoed inside. Whatever was inside knew someone was trespassing on its territory. The pitch black of the darkness inside was consuming, as the brick masonry design wouldn't allow for the smallest leakage of light from outside. Not that the foggy conditions of this night would allow any.

Miniature flashlights, shone by Jackson and Chloe, were the only recourse for visibility. The assorted names and death dates became visible as Chloe pointed her flashlight against the granite grave markers along the mausoleum wall. The sight was unnerving and caused her hands to shake. Jackson's stomach knotted at the thought of his mother and father ending up in a place like this.

The dampened, sour stench of mold and death filled their noses. With slow, deliberate steps, Jackson made his way deeper inside. Chloe clutched the bottom of his shirt as she followed; in lockstep. Jackson felt the warmth of her breath brush against the back of his neck. To Jackson, it felt as though Chloe might crawl inside his skin out of fear. The sound of breaking glass forced Jackson to stall. He turned and pointed his flashlight at his face, widened his eyes, and pressed his index finger on his lips as his remaining fingers clutched the elongated and thick, black rubber object in his hand.

"Do you hear that?" Jackson whispered. His eyes shifted from side to side as he listened.

From the deep darkness in the mausoleum's rear, the faint, repetitive tapping sound reminded Jackson of the pen he nervously tapped against his desk while studying. As Jackson and Chloe ventured deeper inside, the sound grew louder. The tapping stopped, only to be followed by the deepened grunts and groans from something ahead. The moistened sound of ripping flesh mimicked a hungry dog gnawing at a fresh steak given to it by its master. Jackson turned his head and looked back at Chloe, his eyes still widened.

"Pull it," Jackson whispered as he shined the light on the handgun in Chloe's holster. "Keep your distance, and remember what I told you. When I yell, you shine your light on whatever it is back there. Got it?"

Chloe nodded in response. Jackson pushed forward, deeper into the mausoleum. The flashlight pointed at the concrete floor. The reflection of the light as it projected up gave Jackson a wider but still dim illumination ahead. He squinted his eyes and turned his head slightly as he listened. A rapid tapping sound followed by a screeching howl forced Jackson to pause once again. Chloe trailed closely, her flashlight beam wavering as her hand trembled.

Jackson rubbed his thumb on the slightly raised black button on the rubber object in his hand and pressed down. His arm jumped from the recoil of the staggered blade that had ejected from the handle. The clean finish of the silver-plated machete reflected the beams of light from Chloe's flashlight.

Jackson slowly raised his flashlight and found the corner back wall of the crypt. Crimson splatter marks scattered upward along the wall. Jackson followed the blood trail with his flashlight. Chloe's light started on the opposite end, only to meet Jackson's light, which shone on the disfigured creature that stood in front of them. Fresh, blood-colored sores covered its pale, pustulated skin. Its black-tipped fingers clutched the half devoured severed arm of some poor soul that wandered too close in the graveyard. It gnawed down on the flesh and chewed with its blackened, jagged teeth. The creature stopped its feasting briefly, only to chatter its teeth together, producing the tapping sound Jackson and Chloe heard earlier.

Tap, tap, tap, tap.

It turned its head. Its high-pitched, rough snarl filled the air as it stared into the brightness of Jackson and Chloe's flashlights. Its dead, white eyes didn't react to the overexposure of light. As Jackson turned sharply, Chloe's eyes welled up with terror. Looking down, Jackson saw she remained focused on what needed to be done. Her free hand white-knuckled the handle of the handgun in her holster.

He looked back at her and mouthed a singular word . . . *Ghoul.*

The creature stared into the light. Its pale milky white eyes refused to waver. It twisted its skinny frame toward Jackson and grinned at the sight of him. Blood trickled down the corner of its mouth as it indulged in the flesh of some grieving person visiting a grave it had grabbed earlier. A scratchy, high-pitched snarl erupted as the ghoul's black-tipped fingers lunged forward.

Jackson leaped backward. He crashed into Chloe, sending her reeling backward into the granite grave markers. Her flashlight slipped from her hand, hit the ground, and rolled away from her. Its light moved away from its spot on the ghoul and traveled along the wall as it rolled. Jackson avoided the ghoul's clumsy grab and landed a left hook to its jaw. The sour stench of its rot filled Jackson's nostrils. A golf ball sized chunk of the ghoul's softened flesh slid from its jaw and onto the floor.

"Chloe, get up and move back. If it gets its slimy hands on you, it won't let go," Jackson yelled. His voiced echoed inside the small area, filled with panic.

Chloe stood and pulled the handgun from the holster and took several steps back. "Jackson, move! Let me shoot it."

Jackson continued to move in a circular pattern around the ghoul. His hand tightly clutched the wide handle of his retractable machete. The creature moved faster in its attempts to get its hands on Jackson.

I wish the lore of zombies wasn't bullshit. It would be much easier to destroy this twisted monster's brain if it was slow and stupid.

Ghouls were far from slow and stupid. They were much quicker than one would expect. A trait Jackson was also known for, that and his ingenuity.

It reached out again for Jackson's arm as it lunged forward, trying to rip at his flesh. In one motion, Jackson stepped to the side and put his foot out in front of him. The creature tripped over Jackson's foot and stumbled forward toward the back wall of the crypt. Jackson quickly followed as he pushed the ghoul in the back with his forearm and drove it into the wall. The crunch of its facial bones breaking was prominent as its face slammed against the stone. A few of its teeth fell from its mouth. Jackson swung his machete from his waist and plunged it deep into the back of the ghouls skull. The creature's body fell limp to the floor. Jackson stepped on the back of its neck and pulled the machete from its head.

A slight grin appeared on his face as he looked down at the lifeless body of the ghoul. His labored breathing continued, and his hand still gripped the machete firmly.

"Dead. I mean, really dead," Jackson said. His bright smile made its presence.

His thumb pressed the button on the rubber grip of the machete again, and the blade retracted forcefully, causing his arm to jump slightly.

"Are you good, Chloe?" Jackson asked, as he turned his head to look at her, still smiling.

"Not bad for your first time out. How do you feel?"

"I . . . I-I feel," Chloe paused as her timid voice trailed off. She looked back at Jackson and smiled as if she just won one of the gigantic bears at a rigged game at some carnival. "I feel fucking awesome! That was unbelievable. You were so badass, and your machete worked like a charm."

Jackson and Chloe embraced, squeezing tightly, still elated by their intense victory.

"Let's get the hell out of here. The creep factor of this place is off the charts."

Jackson and Chloe made their way back to the front of the mausoleum and pushed open the stone door. Their celebration came to an abrupt halt after Jackson looked up toward his truck and saw the silhouetted figure in front of them. The athletically fit figure donned shoulder length hair. Her hips slightly tilted as her body weight leaned to one side, her hand on that same hip. The more concerning aspect of the silhouetted figure was the large hand cannon clutched in her other hand. Jackson's heart thumped in his chest as the familiar figure walked toward him and Chloe. Her face cleared the fog as she stood only a couple of feet away. Her brow was curled, along with one eyebrow lifted above her right eye. A look of disappointment Jackson was sure he had seen over a thousand times in the past few years.

"Jackson, what the hell are you doing out here with her?"

"Hey, Auntie Nola. How did you know we were here?" Jackson asked, as he turned his head to avoid eye contact.

"I'm a detective, Jackson. It's what I do."

CHAPTER
TWO
"WHAT WERE YOU THINKING BRINGING THAT GIRL WITH YOU ON THAT HUNT?"—NOLA

S unday—Nine days before Mardi Gras Day

There was a saying I had heard a couple of times from my father. Although I can't recall if it was when I was the church-going Catholic girl in my youth, or it it was just something that he said to me in a conversation in my later years.

With age, often comes wisdom.

There were plenty of similar quotes out there, but now that I've passed forty years of age, I'm not sure how wise it was for my ass to get up so early in the morning to pound on a heavy bag. Trauma harmed both my physical and mental well-being. Both were telling me that maybe it was time to quit. Find some peace. Considering everything, I was unsure if peace was readily attainable. Not sure it mattered. Quitting wasn't my style, and there was still a job to do. I just needed to find a release. A way to deal with the trembles and the nightmares.

Honestly, the energetic music and the rhythmic impact of the bag after every kick were still therapeutic. Who was I kidding? It was better than sitting in some stuffy room that reeked of musty leather with stacks of books on the desk and floor. Ten years ago, it would've been what I preferred. These days, I'd much rather exert some energy and frustration in this gym than stick my nose in a book, sitting in my home office.

Memories of Dalyville flashed in my head during my workouts. Four years have passed, but it still haunted me like it was yesterday. Even the heavy bag's pounding couldn't drown out the image of Janice's shriveled body and the lingering smell of formaldehyde that somehow still burned my nostrils and turned my stomach. The more those memories flooded my mind, the harder my fist slammed against that bag. Sweat flew from my brow with every swing.

"You know, if you keep going at that pace, you might sprain your shoulder or something. Those old bones of yours might not hold up." Jackson stood near the door with a bright smile plastered on his face. Strong despite his slender build, he tapped the black collapsible machete's handle against his denim leg.

"I may be older, but I'm sure you don't want me to tune you up with these punches, smart ass," I said with amusement. I unfastened the straps of the boxing gloves with my mouth.

"No, ma'am. I've sparred with you enough to know that you aren't to be messed with. Are you working through some recent night terrors?"

"Yeah, a little bit. I had some horrific flashbacks last night.

Then my encounter with the Grunch earlier that night didn't go as planned," I said.

"You found it? Oh, man! What was it like?" Jackson asked, his eyes shining with excitement.

"It lives up to local legend. The fact that I panicked when it saw me watching it was unexpected and unsettling. I almost screwed up on a simple recon mission. There has to be a way I can manage this PTSD better," I said.

"You'll work through it. It all comes down to finding the right person to talk to. You know, a professional," Jackson said.

"Kid, you are wise beyond your years. So, tell me, why did you do something so dumb?"

Jackson walked a little bit closer and straddled the weight bench in the far corner of the room. His arms rested upon the weight bar. He tilted his head back, his face twisting in anticipation of what was about to happen.

"Okay," he said. "Lay it on me." Jackson shook his head as he braced himself for the lecture.

Adapting to life with a teenage son still took time, even four years later. I guess I should say a young man since his birthday is fast approaching. At twenty years of age he's still temperamental and reckless at moments, Jackson didn't need me to take care of him. The loss of his parents fostered his self-reliance. Hell, at times, I wasn't sure if he was the one taking care of me. Even if that were so, his actions still held consequences.

"What were you thinking, bringing that girl with you to hunt? Chloe can barely defend herself."

"Chloe's not a girl. She's a woman. And you're right, she's not that great at the self-defense part of it yet. But she's smart, and she has great instincts. Chloe is built for this, and the only way she'll learn is by being in the field with us," Jackson said.

His strong feelings for Chloe and hunting were evident in his tone. He meant every word. Whether it was accurate was a different story. They had been together about a year now, and she had shown the fire that was inside her.

"Jackson, I know she helped you design and build Guardian." I nodded my head toward the large black handle in his hand. "You know how deadly ghouls are, and you're right about her being in the field with us if she wants to be a hunter, but a ghoul was an awful choice for her first hunt. They're too hard to kill. Be smarter." I walked closer to him and placed my hands on the weight bar in front of him.

"I designed and built Guardian. The silver coating was her idea. Chloe has value," he said with a crooked smile.

I laughed at his cockiness. He wasn't shy about bragging about his skill set. It fit well with his demeanor. Maybe it was the low-profile Mohawk haircut? Whatever it was, it worked for him.

"I can see what Chloe sees in you and what you see in her. I get it. Your weapon is impressive. You sure you want to call it Guardian? I mean, there are better names, you know. Guardian is pretty corny."

"Auntie, you have Corbin because someone meant something to you. I can't name my badass retractable machete Mom or Dad, right? Guardian sounds a lot better," Jackson said.

"Can't argue with that." I smiled at him and admired how much he had grown over the years since Dalyville. The kid was like a son to me. Something I never thought I would have in this lifetime. In addition, his strength and resilience in the wake of his parents' passing were remarkable, almost unsettling.

"So, usually you have a training partner." Jackson stood, still straddling the bench. "Where's the asshole?" he asked. A stern look and tight lips had replaced his previously prominent smile and soulful, brown eyes. "Let me guess, he's away on business... again."

"Jesus, Jackson. Do we have to do this again? Yes, Charles is away doing some scouting for another acquisition. We should be grateful things have been going well both here in New Orleans and in New York. He has a business to run."

"Four years. It's been four years since Dalyville, and all he does is work. He travels at least once a month, and he doesn't hunt with you anymore. What good is he?"

Jackson glared at me. His voice was a little higher pitched than usual. His disappointed expression was an unexpected gut punch. I wasn't sure if he saw me as weak when it came to Charles. Weakness wasn't a trait I preferred to show to anyone. Not friends or family. Disappointing this kid wasn't high on my priority list, but his assessment of Charles wasn't totally off the mark.

"Jackson, I'm not defending him. Just like us, Charles has endured a great deal. He lost his mother, the only person in this world that loved him, besides Tammy. You and I have each other. He has no one. Let him build his empire. As effective as he is in the field, with or without a weapon, I don't need him to hunt anymore. You and Jordan are the only team I need," I said, walking near the door.

"Charles was supposed to choose us, Auntie. Four years and no mention of a proposal to you... Now he and I barely speak to each other. I don't understand why we need him around at all. We didn't need him in the first place. It should've just been me and you. Since that night, it should've always just been me and you." Jackson's face softened after he spoke. Jackson walked near me.

He was no longer a gangly teenager he once was. Seeing him as a man so early in life was a difficult thing for me. He had to grow up . . . fast. Jackson's early learning curve led him to develop a strong sense of self and the confidence to voice his desires.

"Companionship, Jackson. Charles is around because he offers companionship for me, and I love him. We all share the trauma of losing our parents to something wicked in this world. There aren't many people in our circle that can understand that. That wickedness still lingers out there in the darkness. Charles has done everything he can to be a father figure for you. It's all he talks about when you aren't around."

"I don't need him to be my father. My father is dead, and I'm old enough that I no longer need one. All I need is to know he has your back when I'm not around."

"It doesn't matter how old we get. We always need our parents, or at least a parental figure. I don't know where Charles and I will end up, but what I can assure you is that you're my number one priority," I said.

"Let him go. I don't think he's committed to anything but his business. He hasn't even asked you to marry him after all this time. After everything you two have been through together," Jackson replied.

The jarring ring of my cell phone cut short the uneasy conversation with Jackson. These days, my cell phone was nothing more than a paperweight for the stacks of papers mounted on my desk. Outside of the usual calls from Jackson,

Charles, or Jordan, it was rarely ever used for its intended purpose. My phone screen lit up, displaying 'The Collector,' the contact's name I'd saved four years prior following a brief talk. The sight of the name caused my eyes to widen as I read it.

"Auntie Nola, who's The Collector?" Jackson's brow curled as his eyes darted toward the screen of the ringing phone.

The ringing seemed to get louder and more intense the longer I ignored Jackson's question. I hesitated as I pressed the green circle on the screen.

"What do you want?" I asked after answering.

"Now, now, Nola. Is that anyway to talk to an old friend? We haven't spoken in a while. Don't worry, I've kept my eye on you." The voice on the other end had the tone of a gleeful, articulate man. An individual brimming with self-satisfaction.

"Are you dense? I asked you what you want," I reiterated with a firmer tone.

"All business, I see," the voice paused. "I want you to know that your city has been keeping secrets from you." His voice was smooth and carried a certain elegance I hadn't noticed before, or it was something he kept hidden during his other calls.

"Don't play games with me, asshole. The last time we talked, you threatened me and this city. I'm not interested in your games. You claimed there was a debt owed to you. Come and collect. I'm waiting."

The laughter on the other end of the line irritated me as I sighed.

"As I said before, your city is hiding something from you. I've already started taking what's mine. You just don't know it yet, but you will. Caffin Avenue and Desire Street."

The call abruptly ended, signaled by the sound of a repetitive beeping. Jackson continued to call my name as I regained focus. His brow curled, and his hand extended toward the phone in my hand.

"Jackson, let me tell you about something that occurred on the day I departed Dalyville. I didn't tell you then because you were already going through a lot," I said, exhaling sharply.

"What happened?" Jackson asked.

"A series of cryptic phone calls that harassed me all these years. The one I just received was a little more sinister. A bit different."

"Different how?" Jackson inquired.

"It seems he's here to collect."

CHAPTER
THREE

"DEAD. DRANK HIMSELF TO DEATH."—CAPTAIN TONYA MARTEL

A brief sprint across the backyard to the two-room office building only took a moment or two after my call with the Collector ended. Calling the office space a building was a bit of an exaggeration. It was a small suite addition in the property's rear, but it served its purpose and provided a space for me to keep my work area and living area separate. From the floor beside my desk, I grabbed the black bag and stuffed it with some extra weapons hanging on the wall nearby. I slid the cool, soft leather of Corbin's holster over my shoulders and snapped it in. I texted Jordan and Charles and advised them of the location given to me by the voice on the other end of the line.

"Meet me in the Lower Ninth Ward. Caffin Avenue and Desire Street."

"Jordan, reach out to your contact in the police department. Let them know we have a body at Caffin Avenue and Desire Street. It looks like this one could be of a supernatural nature."

The overpowering stench of a decaying body that clashed jarringly with the otherwise pleasant smell of wildflowers and overgrown grass sickened and angered me. The tip given by the creep on the other end of the phone was accurate. A woman was lying lifeless before me. Her chest had a softball-sized hole where her heart used to be. She spent her last moments on an abandoned plot of land, dying . . . alone. There was a tragic irony to the scene. In a once-thriving community, destroyed and rotting homes stood abandoned and dilapidated, consumed by the overgrown grass and winding vines. A neighborhood washed away by a storm and left behind by society to die. Something did the same to this woman. Destroyed by a force and left to die. Her appearance triggered a flurry of thoughts in my mind.

It's real.

At least from this piece of evidence, the mystery man on the other end of those calls was real. The body, coupled with the information, proved his gravity—he wasn't a prank caller who had tormented me for years. Instead of some fanboy's harassment, it was the Collector's true intentions that filled me with worry. What the hell did he want?

Jordan finished his call and stood next to me as I stared at the lifeless body and its details. Her face was flawless. Her pale skin and closed eyes gave the impression of a peaceful rest. Except for the gaping chest wound and missing throat, the body could have been easily mistaken for someone simply sleeping. Jordan dry heaved at the gruesome sight of the mutilation. Charles, in his ever-distracted state, seemed to mostly ignore the poor woman lying before him. The cell phone welded to his hand completely consumed his attention.

"I reached out to my contact like you asked. He said the city received the same anonymous phone call with a lot more detail. The caller stated that the suspects are on the scene right now. This is the third body in thirty days with similar wounds," Jordan said.

"What? Someone is trying to set us up," I said, eyes darted in Jordan's direction.

"Not only that, but there were also other deaths. The wounds were much more savage. Much more brutal, also probably caused by something supernatural," Jordan answered.

"Jordan, I'm confused. Why would the city choose to keep these murders from me? From what you've said, the deaths were obviously unusual in nature. I don't understand."

"Apparently, there's some hotshot captain that has been working out of headquarters for the past year. She seems to have a lot of pull and convinced the brass of NOPD to keep this in house and away from you. I didn't think much of it because I didn't have all the details. Just figured it was another murder in the streets of New Orleans. That is, until I laid eyes on it myself."

"Well, I've never seen a wound like that before. From the looks of it, someone was either very skilled with a scalpel, or possibly working in the medical profession. Still, there's something off about this," I said.

Charles continued his ferocious texting spree as his thumbs rapidly moved across the screen of his phone. His eyes darted at the lifeless body only a few feet away from him, then right back to his phone. The sight of that poor woman that lay stiff and pale so close to him seemed to have zero effect. Charles stood focused on whatever it was he was doing, eventually turning his back to us. It was no way for any hunter to behave.

"Are we boring you, Charles?" I asked as I walked up behind him and turned him to face me.

"Far from bored. I know this type of mystery is right up your alley. I'm sure you and your little boy toy over there will find whatever murdered this poor woman. Right now, I have a wealthy investor in town, and I need to give him my undivided attention. There's too much at stake," Charles said.

"Boy toy? I think you should watch who you're talking to. I'm here to have Nola's back. That's a lot more than I could say about you," Jordan asserted, squaring his shoulders in Charles' direction.

Jordan's build wasn't that much smaller than Charles. Both stood about the same height, with Charles just a bit more muscular. His experiences as a homicide detective, including encounters with the city's toughest individuals, led Jordan to react strongly to any disrespect shown to him or his colleagues.

Charles ignored the bravado pointed in his direction from Jordan and looked me directly in the eyes. His shoulders slumped as his eyes widened with regret.

"Nola, I have to leave town for a couple of days. I need to go to New York for a while. I promise I'll—"

The blaring of police sirens fast approaching drew my attention as Charles continued to ramble. With tires screeching, three police cars slid to a stop just short of us. A pair of police officers exited each vehicle to the left and right, surrounding the abandoned plot of land with yellow caution tape.

An androgynously dressed person stepped out of the center vehicle, leaving the door ajar. The officer's soft facial features were at odds with her attire: navy blue cargo pants, a police T-shirt, and a baseball cap, which projected a powerful image. The police officer's face was partly concealed by her glasses. It wasn't until she came a little closer that I realized it was a woman. The person's curled brow and flared nostrils indicated they weren't interested in a pleasant conversation. Her pants shifted around her plump waist and her gold badge glistened as it bathed in the sunlight. Her gaze held firm in my direction.

"Nola Maor, I presume? It's definitely not a pleasure to meet you and your merry band of idiots." The captain glared at the three of us above her glasses.

The frames were of a style I had never seen before. A putrid shit colored brown that lacked any presence or style. The captain's short, quick strides came to a stop as she took out her notepad and immediately began to take notes. As she approached, her face jogged my memory. Familiar, but she was still unknown to me. The smile plastered on her face as she stared at us wasn't one of joy but of satisfaction. That was a smile I had seen plenty of times before, years ago, as a detective.

"Nola Maor, Eric Jordan, and Charles Jones. What, Jackson too busy to contaminate a crime scene and interfere with a police investigation?" the captain asked with a smile still present.

"Do I know you?" I replied.

"We've never officially met, but you've heard of me, and you worked with my father. I'm Captain Tonya Martel."

"Chief Martel's daughter? The one he bragged about all the time as the love of his life? How has he been?"

"Dead. Drank himself to death after getting his pension and job stripped away. Of course, you would know that if you had bothered to come around and check on the man that went to bat for you and what you did behind the scenes for the city."

"I—I was just focused on keeping the city safe," I stammered.

"What are you doing here? Some time ago, homicide units were taken from the individual precincts and was centralized at police headquarters. I'm in charge of that unit and this very special one. I didn't have anyone notify you, and the city has been gradually phasing you and your activities out, if you hadn't noticed. Who called you?"

The other officers ignored us, walked past the caution tape, and kneeled by the corpse. Jordan glared in my direction to get my attention and nodded at the officers as two of them popped open black briefcases in front of them. They removed tools I hadn't seen before when I was on the force. Come to think of it, there was nothing normal about how they handled the scene.

"I have my sources, Captain. Do you have any idea what you could be dealing with here? This can't be the first murder with this M.O. if you came out to this scene yourself. Why wasn't I brought in on this and why aren't there more officers and a crime lab out here?" I asked. My brow curled with confusion.

Charles had the nerve to insert himself in between me and Captain Martel. He glared at me, and his upper lip curled.

"We need to leave," Charles said.

"Ms. Maor, I know exactly what we could be dealing with. This team you're looking at is the city's new S.N.S. team. It's a supernatural squad if you will. We do the studying. We do the hunting. You, Nola, are unnecessary." Captain Martel stepped around Charles and walked a little closer to me.

"Once we hunt down whatever was responsible for this, the city will put an end to your little supernatural private investigation agency. Once the city is done with you, I'll dedicate my time to putting your ass in jail for the rest of your life. Or I'll put a bullet in you myself. Right now, I would do as your meathead boyfriend advised and get the hell off my scene. This isn't your concern." Captain Martel averted her gaze toward the officers kneeling next to the body, doing her best to ignore my existence.

"A threat to my life? So, you're a badge bully. Here's a piece of advice, Martel. That badge won't protect you against the things you might come across. Tread carefully. Let's go, Jordan. We'll investigate this on our end," I said, turning my back to Martel. I ensured my voice reached her. "Charles, don't you have a flight to catch? Go. Take care of your business. Jordan and I will handle this."

Stunned by my reaction, Charles stood with his mouth open like an idiot. Sometimes I wondered if he knew me at all. When it came to disrespecting each other, this was the first time we had both ventured into those waters. Despite his brutality as a hunter, Charles had always showed me kindness and respect. This was the first time I was dismissive of him. I wasn't sure if Jackson got in my head or not, but I didn't feel good about it. Charles had never shown any violent tendencies toward me, but I had never put him in this situation before. I'm not sure he could handle me, let alone me and Jordan. Jordan had become quite the skilled fighter since he joined our ranks. I wasn't sure what was going on with him, but I was sure that whatever he was going through would be a distraction. He needed to leave.

"I need to do this. I'm not trying to get in your way, Nola. I love you, but this is important," Charles said, exhaling sharply as he turned and walked away.

"Then go! Do your business," I yelled.

"Uh oh, trouble in paradise?" Captain Martel asked with a chuckle.

I wanted nothing more than to punch that smug look off her face.

"I'll be in touch, Captain. I don't take threats lightly."

CHAPTER
FOUR
"I SEE YOU, CHARLES. WHAT ARE YOU DOING OUT HERE?"—JACKSON

Monday—Eight days before Mardi Gras

Jackson's hands tensed around the steering wheel of the truck as he trailed the car in front of him. The low position of the sun as dusk set in made it difficult for Jackson to gauge his distance. In the quiet, low-income neighborhood, his smooth idling technique allowed him to follow without the truck's engine constantly revving—a police technique taught to him by Nola. A passed technique that became handy when needed. The dark-colored sedan a couple hundred yards in front rolled cautiously on the narrow roadway of the trashy and mostly abandoned neighborhood. Debris and discarded old tires almost completely covered the littered median and sidewalk flanking the pothole-riddled road. A brilliant orange hue in the sky highlighted the towering Ferris wheel as Jackson's sightline cleared the surrounding trees. Even from the road, Jackson could make out the peeled and cracked paint on the amusement park's carousel and rollercoaster. Some of the passenger cars of the rides dangled loose, only held on by a single bolt. The dilapidated wooden framed rollercoaster which shared the skyline with the Ferris wheel was a ghost of a past New Orleans that Jackson never had the opportunity to enjoy. There were only remnants of fond memories shared with him by his mother.

"I guess your instincts were right, babe. Why in the hell would he be coming out here to an old, abandoned amusement park?" Chloe asked.

"I have no idea. Once Aunt Nola told me he was headed to New York on business, I gave Tammy a call. She runs the New York office, and if he was going there, then she would know."

"Since we're following Charles, I take it Tammy didn't know he was coming?" Chloe asked.

"Exactly. There were no pressing matters, according to her, and she would know. So, I've been keeping my eyes on him all day. What I do know is that his ass is lying to my Aunt Nola. He should have been in New York since yesterday," Jackson answered.

"What do you think he's up to?" Chloe asked.

Jackson leaned forward, squinting as Charles' vehicle slowed down.

"Aunt Nola called and told me he was acting like a weirdo yesterday. Told me he was distracted on a scene and was a bit disrespectful toward her. I've never heard her say that before about him. Figured I better find out what he was hiding. Looks like I was right," he said.

"So, what's the plan?" Chloe asked.

"It looks like he's headed inside the old amusement park. I'm going to follow him on foot. You stay here with the car running . . . just in case. I'm putting in my earbuds and calling you now. I'll keep you on the line and updated on what I see while on the phone."

The truck rolled to a stop on the side of the road after Jackson shifted to neutral, cut the engine, and let it drift. Charles drove up to the entrance, jumped out of the car, and unlocked the chain wrapped around the gate. He often looked behind him with caution. The last remnants of the sun barely peeked above the thick cluster of clouds on the horizon, as Charles drove past the rusted, gated entrance. Jackson watched Charles drive further into the park toward the severely damaged ticket and management office. He followed on foot.

"Well, this isn't the airport. Black cargo pants and tactical gear aren't Charles' style for business meetings," Jackson whispered.

He looked around and noticed the mold-covered walls adorned with painted cartoon alligators and music notes. The towering colorful amusement rides in the nearby distance made him wonder what joys he could have experienced with his parents provided by this park when it thrived. Now it was only filled with desolate and forgotten spaces.

The abandoned theme park was once a popular destination in New Orleans for families and members of the community. Scorned after missing out on what turned out to be the most popular theme park in the world, which eventually landed in Florida, the city of New Orleans finally managed to build its own land of adventure. Only to be washed away by one of the most devastating storms in the Crescent City's history years later. Now it sat rusted and rotted.

Covered in mold with bits of the land already swallowed again by nature, the passing wind carried the faint echoes of children's laughter. Weeds had grown and slithered their way over passenger cars of rides and up the sides of structures that stood clinging to their last bolt.

Squinting, Jackson attempted to adjust to his darkened surroundings as he ventured deeper into what was nothing more than a ghost town. Without working power lines or a functional lamp post, it was difficult to see his own hand in front of him. The sound of crashing objects, like empty paint cans hitting the pavement, suggested Charles was inside the building ahead. The only way to be sure was for Jackson to make his way a little closer. Hell, for all he knew, it could have been some nocturnal critters that made their nest inside the dilapidated structure simply rummaging through garbage. After all, Jackson wasn't quite sure where Charles ducked off to after he parked his car. Charles moved quick enough that even Jackson had trouble staying close to him as he tried to track him. Even with the blackness of the night, Jackson did not want to use his cell phone flashlight app to give away his position. The last thing Jackson wanted was for Charles to see him. Light not only deterred the nocturnal, but it also attracted it, and often, the wrong type of creature.

"Do you smell anything?" Chloe asked. Her voice came in loud and clear in Jackson's earbuds.

The unexpected sound of Chloe's voice sent a quick jolt down his spine and caused him to turn and hit his head against the side of the ticket booth. Jacksons rubbed the side of his head as he winced in pain.

"Chloe, you just scared the shit out of me. I forgot you were there."

Chloe giggled on the other end of the phone, obviously

taking some pleasure in the thought of scaring the self-proclaimed badass hunter.

"Stay alert, tough guy," Chloe said as she continued to giggle.

"What the heck kinda question was that, anyway? Do I smell anything? Yep. I smell mildew and garbage," Jackson said, irritated at the question.

"Jackson, enough jokes. I need you to focus. You know, being aware of your senses is the first step in hunting. You taught me that. Charles loves his colognes, right? If you don't smell it, either you aren't close enough or he's not wearing any. He doesn't wear any when he's hunting. If he's pursuing prey, what is he hunting and why is he doing it alone?" Chloe said.

Jackson grinned as he listened to her. "Damn it, woman, this is the reason I love you. So damn smart."

"That's not the only reason you love me," Chloe replied. Jackson's grin grew a little larger.

"I don't get it. I know he hasn't been upfront with Aunt Nola, but why is he out here? This place has remained abandoned for years. It looks like he went into the far end of the park, into a building that says, 'Guest Services'," Jackson said.

Jackson sprinted across the open area, kicked an empty soda can on his way to the guest services structure, and squatted down beneath the shattered window. The unexpected clang of rattling tin caused the soft red hue that emanated from the shattered window to flash from side to side from inside. As the clouds cleared, Jackson looked up and saw a brightly lit full moon casting light across the night sky.

"I know it's you, Charles. Why are you out here?" Jackson mumbled. A deafening silence followed.

Jackson crawled with caution to the corner of the window.

He removed the weighty rubber handle of the Guardian from his waist holster and slowly peered over the corner of the windowsill. The pungent odor of the moldy wood filled his nostrils. Jackson held his breath to not make a sound.

Charles sat inside and read what appeared to be a journal of some sort. It didn't appear old, at least not older than twenty or thirty years old. How he could read anything in this darkness, even with that red flashlight, was beyond Jackson. Charles' favorite sawed-off double-barrel shotgun lay beside him as he read. The remaining area inside was full of an assortment of leftover damaged debris from the storm and graffiti. Except—there was one other item that sat in the far corner of the desk. A familiar nylon gym bag, which Jackson had seen countless times in Charles' hand.

"Jackson, I need an update. Did you find him? What's he doing? Are you okay?" Chloe's soft voice asked the rapid-fire questions in Jackson's ear. His hand covered his ear to muffle the noise.

Jackson settled into a spot near the outside corner of the structure that kept him both comfortable, out of sight, and able to keep his eyes on Charles for as long as needed. The creaking of metal from a riding car on a nearby kiddy attraction drew Jackson's attention. The squeaky noise was followed by an unexpected howl echoing through the night air. Jackson's eyes shifted in the direction of the howl briefly, and darted them back toward Charles, who was now on his feet, also peering in the direction of the howl. Chloe's voice was lost to Jackson, who could only hear his heart pounding in his ears. Jackson had never heard a howl like that before. Somehow, he knew it wasn't simply a dog or a swamp coyote. The howl was deeper and more visceral than any domestic animal he had ever heard.

Fear consumed Jackson's legs as he remained motionless. Jackson almost immediately understood the reality of what made that howl. A plummeting sensation in the pit of his stomach followed.

Charles darted out of the condemned office. He stood with the shotgun in hand, pointing into the darkness. A deep primal growl crept from the depth of the blackness. Jackson continued to duck behind the building and watched as Charles slowly walked closer toward the growl.

As the obscure, animal-shaped shadow reached further into the park, the faded yellow and green child's ride shook violently. Jackson watched as Charles gave chase with only his gun in hand, reckless in his hunt.

"What the hell are you doing?" Jackson mumbled. His eyes expanded as his breathing became shallow with fear. The feeling in his legs returned, and the surrounding area again fell silent.

"You're on your own, you fucking liar," Jackson said as he turned his flashlight app on and ran for the park entrance. "Chloe, I'm fine. I'm on my way back to the car. Charles was out here hunting. I think he was hunting a werewolf."

CHAPTER
FIVE
"AUNTIE NOLA, WHERE'S CHARLES?"—JACKSON

Tuesday—Seven days before Mardi Gras

Although something about the cold temperature was comforting, it was difficult to come by in New Orleans. A cold shower was my refuge. The cool water caressed my body, horrific images of the blistered skin and massive teeth of Goliath and the pupil-less blackened sunken sockets of the banshee plagued my thoughts. Of course, the piercing red eyes, size, and strength of the lycanthrope that killed my parents accompanied them. The memories of them remained clear, as if they were standing in front of me. With trembling hands, I shut off the shower, trying to control my breathing.

"Water wasn't cold enough, I guess," I whispered, my breath still uneven.

Water dripped from my body onto the shaggy carpet under my feet. As I wiggled my toes deeper into the fabric, the cool air from the air-conditioning vent brushed against my moist skin. The chills that covered me were a welcome refreshment. I centered myself and gazed into the body length mirror mounted on the wall in front of my naked body. My body exhibited the visible marks of the trauma I'd suffered. I turned my back toward the mirror and peered over my shoulder to view the deep scars that stretched the length of my back, courtesy of Goliath. My fingers ran along the gash in my thigh inflicted by the banshee. I faced the mirror, leaning in to rub the deep pencil length scar from that cursed werewolf, the most terrible of them all. The daily, ever-present reminder of my failure. The sight of the scar became hazy as water filled my eyes.

"Christ, get your shit together, Nola. There's no time for this today," I mumbled, reaching for the clothes nearby. "Jordan is waiting for me."

The chime of the doorbell was incredibly irritating. Whom ever it was had impeccable timing. Dropping my clothes back on the chair, I rushed to the door as fast as I could to not keep whomever it was waiting. I had the reputation of being the weirdo on the block. I stayed to myself, and I knew how that could be perceived. Being labeled as the weirdo in the neighborhood wouldn't help when I needed information on anything that could be going on in the city, but I had managed to work around the stigma.

The doorbell rang again as I rushed to the door with the towel barely wrapped around my unmentionables. I opened the door, and the widow Mrs. Bradley stood there doing her best to look around me as she tried to peek inside.

"Hey there, Nola. I noticed you parked your car a little

closer to the front of my house and my driveway than usual. If you brought in your garbage cans, you could park in front of your own door. You could have that chocolate man of yours take care of it. I'm sure he's capable. I watch him do the yard work all the time."

Mrs. Bradley's husband died a couple of years ago. She was such a sweet old lady before his passing. A little nosey, though. I thought the loss of her husband had sent her over the edge a bit. Couldn't really blame her for that.

"Thanks, Mrs. Bradley. I'll be sure to bring them in. Have you been watching over the neighborhood again? You know we need you to make sure everything is in order around here," I said, hitching up the towel that seemed to do its best to fall off me.

"Damn right I am. Mr. Benson, the Richards, and even that hussy in the house on the other side of me have been running around, coming and going at all times of the night. They're nothing but a bunch of heathens."

I slightly closed the door to shield my partially exposed body from onlookers.

"Well, Mrs. Bradley, it's Mardi Gras season. They're probably just enjoying the festivities."

"I don't care what they're doing. It's dangerous out there, and if you're leaving at all times of the night, then you're up to no good. Bunch of damn heathens. I hope the monster bites them in the ass." Mrs. Bradly smacked herself on her rear and stared at the towel, her lips pursed.

"That's not nice. What do you know about the monster running around here?" I asked.

"I know enough. I've heard things. My bingo club has all

kinds of people in it. Like Mr. Allen, he has a son in the police department, and he told me that there have been people getting killed. Bodies just ripped apart. The city just doesn't want to tell nobody. Seein' that it's Mardi Gras and all."

"Is that right?" I asked.

"That's right. And I know you're having a party for that sweet boy of yours. When is it?"

Mrs. Bradley's insight was downright creepy sometimes. She stood there with her brow raised with a look of satisfaction.

"The party is in a couple of days. I was going to invite you. It wouldn't be a party without you. Until then, make sure you stay inside at night until it all blows over," I said, as I nudged the door closed a little more.

"I don't need you telling me what to do. You just let me know when's that boy's party. I'll bake him a pie. Go and put some clothes on. Nobody's interested in lookin at your goodies." Mrs. Bradley turned and started down the stairs of the porch.

I quickly closed the door, rested my head upon it, and exhaled sharply.

"Hussy," Mrs. Bradley's voice carried from the other side of the door.

Eyes closed, I let out a deep sigh. "That woman is exhausting."

Cars zipped through the intersection while I sat on the trunk of the parked car near the corner. The foot traffic was unbelievably busy, something that would rival the busiest cross streets in any major city. The intersection of State Avenue and Community Street was the home of two massive stone buildings—the police headquarters and the criminal courthouse—whose sole intent was to dole out justice for the city of New Orleans and the State of Louisiana. I was no longer that twenty-two-year-old naïve police detective. There was no justice in this city, or anywhere, for that matter. There was only good and evil, and there was no doubt that evil had this world by the throat. Its bloody claws relentlessly applied pressure. When I committed to this lifestyle, I thought it was the best way I could prevent tragedy before it happened. Most times I succeeded. The few times I didn't, someone paid the price with their life. Sometimes I think I bit off more than I could chew. Ironically, there was less self-doubt when I was a young cop.

Jordan hustled out of the police headquarters, a yellow file in hand, and made his way through the bustling intersection. His smile was easily visible from the other side of the street. Jordan's smile and charm were only superseded by his integrity and his intellect. It didn't hurt that he was easy on the eyes. After all those years of being my eyes and ears on the street as a Homicide Detective, I never would have expected him to leave the force and work with me. I tried to tempt him on so many occasions. His commitment to the police department seemed unwavering. Until it wasn't. Jordan never discussed why he decided to help me hunt. I'm just grateful that he did.

"Nola, smart move leaking the body we found to the press. Once the news broke the story, I had no problem getting the information we needed. Secrets out, and the brass are trying to cover their asses. My contact inside advised that you stay away from headquarters." Jordan raised his brow and the yellow file in his hand. "I found out two interesting things. First, that asshole captain on the scene running the hunter unit for the police department... I can confirm that's Captain Martel, as in Chief Martel's daughter. I know you had your doubts about if that was the same little girl you saw in the pictures he showed you, but she is."

"That explains why she has so much hatred for me. Chief never forgave me for spilling the beans on his Deacon Bianchi fairytale. I just couldn't live with that lie anymore," I said.

Jordan curled his brow and anxiously scratched one of his eyebrows while gritting his teeth. "You cost him his career, Nola. Her father died without his pension as a disgrace of the department. You can't blame her. I'd be pissed with you too," Jordan replied.

Lowering my head, I sighed, unable to argue against his point. It wasn't my best decision. The Chief did what he thought was best for the department. My decision to rat him out, on the other hand, well, I'll admit that was selfish. Leave it to Jordan to call me out on my bullshit. Charles would have let it go.

"What else?" I said sharply, cutting my eyes back toward Jordan.

"The second thing is that the poor woman with her heart ripped out wasn't the first in the city. She was the fourth. From what my contact said, Captain Martel is working with the upper brass to lock you out."

"Doesn't matter. Eventually, we were going to run across this. What makes them think they can lock us out? The

Collector is causing this somehow. Hell, he led us to her, and if it fits his twisted agenda, then he'll lead us to others," I replied.

"I think . . . " He paused. "What happened yesterday was what Captain Martel was waiting on. Catching us on a scene standing next to a dead body. From what I gather, we're all under investigation now. Not because they think you did it, but because they can use it to make others think you did, and eventually put all of us behind bars."

"Christ . . . " I replied, rolling my eyes. "Something's gonna have to be done about her. There's enough to deal with without worrying about some overzealous cop with a personal vendetta."

"Anyway, the other three bodies had the same M.O. Flesh, muscle, and bone all surgically cut away with precision and then their hearts violently ripped out from their bodies. Torn vessels and arteries. Their hearts were never found."

Extending my hand for the file in Jordan's hands, my mind raced at the possible types of creatures that had a fetish for human hearts. Nothing immediately came to mind.

"Were the victims all women?" I asked, looking down at the files.

"Nope. Both male and female. The last page shows a thirty-year-old math teacher. Male," Jordan replied.

"Are the four victims connected somehow?"

"No connections found by the department."

"Jordan, whatever is doing this has a tremendous amount of self-control and an unhealthy amount of rage all at the same time. The skill it would take to cut this deep . . . then have enough power to rip out the heart? This is new," I said. My brow tensed as I shook my head in disbelief.

"Worried? You? I don't think I've ever seen that look on

your face before," Jordan said with a crooked smile. "Still cute though."

I cut my eyes at Jordan. One eyebrow raised. I tried my best to suppress the smile his sly remark caused. Unsuccessful, I could feel the tension on my cheeks. I winked at Jordan in return.

I can't believe I did that.

The mid-day sun shone intensely down on the bustling downtown area as I stood from the trunk of my car. I squinted, shielding my face with my hand.

"I think it's best that we get to work on figuring out what's doing this. We need to be prepared for everything."

The chair creaked. It wiggled and leaned to the point that I could barely tolerate sitting in it. I've sat behind this desk and in this chair so much it was no longer comfortable. It irritated me. On top of it all, I read through the police reports again and another one of the many books on the occult from my library. I was no closer than before. The more I read, the more frustration set in as I came up empty-handed. Not a creature, demon, or poltergeist was documented to feed on human hearts. Nothing by any past hunter or occultist was recorded with that precision when it feasted or killed. At least, none that I found.

There was no doubt that my sister, Janice, would've had a clear understanding of what or who was doing this by now. I had done my best to live up to who she was, the type of hunter she was. I kept my home office freezing cold to mimic her, although the cold temperature wasn't ideal for me all the time. It helped me focus somehow, prevented the panic attacks.

Janice, I miss you so much.

"Oh, why did I quit drinking?" I mumbled.

Alcohol was no longer in the picture. Those days I spent intoxicated compromised my investigative skills and would one day keep me from being there for someone who needed me. Someone like Jackson or Charles. I couldn't take that chance. So, a little mindless scrolling on social media made for a great distraction from the frustration. Cell phone in hand, I pressed down on the blue-colored app and scrolled through my timeline. Picture after picture, and every stupid post updating the world on what they had for dinner. So many associates of mine appeared to have perfect lives. No struggle. No strife. Just joy and families they had nurtured for years. I wouldn't call them friends or family. Those titles were only for the select few that remained in my life. The ones I hadn't let down. This app and a fake profile picture allowed me to keep tabs on them from afar.

Visions of selfie after selfie and inappropriate memes induced a small chuckle now and then. The posts from some past faces still on the police department were curious and cryptic in nature and quickly changed the vibe of my timeline. Cryptic post about the new tasks-force and their ability to handle these types of murders were pushed to my feed. Some didn't have as much faith. The smile on my face was fleeting as headlines from the news sources I followed made their way into the algorithm.

"Mutilated body found in Algiers."

"Gruesome dismembered body of New Orleans, man discovered. Shades of Goliath."

"Bywater woman violently murdered. Neighbors fear Goliath's return."

The name Goliath in print again flooded my head with memories I had effectively compartmentalized deep inside, for the most part. There was no doubt Goliath did its damage to its victims, and the acts were brutal and filled with rage. The scars on my back proved it. From the descriptions in the articles, the wounds inflicted were violent like Goliath, but these were messy. I would say primal. All of these . . . things had a certain way they inflicted pain on the human body. Vampires, ghouls, banshees, lycanthropes . . . They each had an M.O., and these differed greatly from the surgical precision murders that happened. This couldn't be what I thought it was. I killed almost all of them that called New Orleans home. Then I ran the remaining ones out of town. There were no werewolves left here.

The unexpected opening of the front door startled me. Jackson walked around the immediate adjacent wall and into the living room, where I had set up a makeshift office for the night. He stood and stared at me. His eyes widened and his mouth slightly opened as if he was struggling to tell me something he had held in for a long time. The look in his eyes made me uncomfortable with the anticipation of what he was holding back. Jackson wasn't the dramatic type. Never was. Whatever was going on, he didn't like it.

"Auntie, where's Charles?" Jackson blurted out.

"He's still out of town on business. He should be back tomorrow. Why do you ask?" I replied.

"No. No, he's not. I saw him yesterday. Here in the city."

I stood from the sofa; my brow curled in confusion.

"Jackson, you must be mistaken. Charles can't be in town. He had to meet a client in New York."

Because if he was in town, then that would make him a liar. I hate liars.

"I don't know why he lied to you, but it was definitely him. I tracked him down to the abandoned amusement park after dark, but that wasn't all. He had some sort of makeshift office set up and . . . there was a werewolf, I think," Jackson said. He swallowed tentatively as he stared down at the expression of rage on my face.

I walked closer to Jackson. He stood in front of me with his shoulders slumped. His body language told me that he was nervous, but his face said that there was more. Jackson's apprehension might have been plastered all over his face, but based on his recent history and his feelings about Charles, I was sure he'd spill whatever else he had to say.

"Are you sure, Jackson? I ran them all out of town or put them in the ground. Lycanthropes should know better than to lay roots here."

"I'm sure. Charles was there, and he was armed. I heard the howl of a wolf. Charles ran off into the night at the abandoned park when he heard it too. It had to be a werewolf. It was a full moon," Jackson replied.

"It doesn't matter if it was a full moon or not. It depends on what type of were—"

The sound of a howl outside in the night air interrupted. The sound was like the sudden screech of nails on a chalkboard, prominent from the backyard. Jackson and I rushed to the back porch, down the stairs, and into the yard. I held Corbin instinctively in my hand as I scanned the backyard, its barrel pointed with an intent to bury a silver bullet in the flesh of anything that wandered around on my property. As we turned around and scanned the back of the house, the deep impressions of four collective scratches that ran parallel along the back door caused my heart to beat violently in my chest and a tingle ran down my spine.

"Jackson, I believe you."

CHAPTER SIX

"WHY ARE YOU FOLLOWING ME? WHO TOLD YOU I WAS IN TOWN?"—CHARLES

The patrons differed from what I remembered. A few weeks ago, Charles conveyed to me it wasn't like before. He was entirely aware of what it was like after I shared so many of my police stories with him. The charming gourmet coffee shop was built on the corner of a peculiar triangular block of land. It used to be a makeshift satellite station for detectives of the first precinct. In our conversations, I'd tell Charles how most of my coworkers would get together and do everything from brainstorming open cases to bitching about our significant others. It was the optimal place, away from district leadership and in an aesthetically pleasing neighborhood.

The triangular building sat in the middle of a stretch of city blocks where towering oak trees aligned like standing dominoes on both sides of the street. The massive roots of the trees had punched through the paved sidewalks and created a chaotic walkway with broken and elevated fragments of concrete. In contrast, the trees offered great shade during summer and were comfortable in fall. Those things hadn't changed. What had changed was the clientele. Before, an assortment of city workers with badges frequented the coffee shop, and now it was overrun with a steady rotation of hipsters wearing flip-flops and cardigan sweaters.

I hated to admit it, but Charles was right. This was my type of place, yet as I sat and watched him hold a conversation with some older white man sitting next to him, all I could think about was breaking his nose.

Why lie to me? What are you hiding?

The man that sat with Charles held his recycled cardboard coffee cup and laughed as they conversed. Dressed in a well-tailored navy-blue suit accented with a golden yellow tie, he appeared to be a business executive of some sort. He had a full head of salt-and-pepper colored hair combed to one side and parted down the other side of his head. Everything about him exuded wealth and privilege. Charles looked like he belonged in his company, wearing his own perfectly tailored mahogany brown suit. Their posture was flawless as they sat. If I didn't know Charles any better, I would think they were the model corporate douchebag types.

He's been lying to you, Nola. Do you really know him at all?

I strapped Corbin into its holster and tightened the straps around my shoulder, so the heavy framed sidekick wouldn't shift too much as I moved. A quick jog across the street, then I traversed the busy roadway. Charles spotted me. His eyes widened as I approached them. Charles stood in shock, adjusting his tie and suit jacket, while averting his eyes away from mine. The Caucasian man next to him face contorted with confusion. My eyes burned, brimming with vitriol. I inhaled deeply to wrestle in my fury.

"I see you're doing well, Charles. Must have been a twelve-hour emergency turnaround trip to New York. Your knees and fingers are all fully functional . . . for now." I glared at him. "Is there a reason you didn't use those fingers to call and tell me you were back in town?"

"Nola, I can explain. I—,"

I turned my shoulders away from Charles and focused on the man that sat with him. I was unsure why he had to lie or how many times Charles had lied about leaving town on business, but I figured the man next to him might have some answers considering how friendly the two of them looked. He wasn't what I expected from afar. Much skinnier up close, but despite his salt-and-pepper colored hair, he could still pass for someone in their forties. Although, the way he carried himself, I believed he was older.

"And you are?" I asked, extending my hand, staring him in his crystal blue eyes.

"Hello, I'm Frank Lopez, associate and potential business partner of Mr. Jones, depending on how things fall into place."

Charles set his hand on my shoulder and turned me back to face him. His face was no longer filled with angst from being caught in his lie. Charles' body language shifted to a more confrontational demeanor.

"Why are you following me? Who told you I was in town?" Charles asked.

"I'm a detective, Charles. No one told me. You're not as smart as you think you are. Why the hell do you have to lie about leaving town for business?" My face warmed as blood rushed to it.

Charles smirked at my little jab at his intelligence and nodded. "Mr. Lopez was the business I was referring to. I'm not getting into why I misled you right now, but I need you to trust me and just leave, right now. I'm conducting business." Charles smirked. His attempt to keep up appearances in front of Frank, no doubt.

The large vein in his neck bulged and throbbed as his body tensed. Watching him react to being caught in a lie with anger and denial infuriated me.

I closed my hand firmly into a fist, panting at his audacity. "What the hell do you mean, I need me to leave?"

"Umm, g-guys..." Frank stuttered.

"Nola, just leave, woman! Why are females so damn hard-headed?" Charles yelled.

"I know you didn't just say . . . " My eyebrow raised at Charles' words.

Frank stood; his eyes widened. His arm, along with his slightly wrinkled, pale hand and index finger, shot out. "W-what the h-hell is that?" he stuttered.

Both Charles and I turned in the direction Frank pointed. One of the few gaps in the tree line that allowed a significant amount of sunlight through fell right above the direction in which Frank pointed. The glare of the sun partially obstructed most of the oak tree, which was the only object in the direction Frank's shaky hand pointed. This tree was oddly shaped and slightly discolored along its edge on one side. There was no part of any oak tree that had black fur, unnaturally large biceps, and what appeared to be clawed fingers. The creature did a poor job of concealing itself, with more than half of its massive frame exposed beyond the cover of the tree. Worse, maybe its intent was to be seen.

As I squinted to get a clearer look, its features became prominent. The disfigured, pointed ears and elongated snout were almost as grotesque as its massive canine teeth, long arms, and pointed, discolored claws, which hung near its knees.

My heart pounded violently in my chest, and hands shook uncontrollably. My skin turned cold.

No way in hell. Not now. I don't need this right now.

"Nola, are you seeing this?" Charles said.

I couldn't steady my hand as I clumsily reached for Corbin to free it from my holster. Pull after pull, the holster shifted, and Corbin refused to free itself. A brief glance down revealed the strap from my holster entwined around the hammer of Corbin. I dropped to a knee and pulled the backup gun from my ankle holster.

The beast, in open stride on all four limbs, made its way across the street in what seemed like less than a blink of an eye. Its teeth moistened with saliva the entire time.

I took aim to fire before it could reach the crowd of screaming people now scrambling to escape a painful and bloody death. I lined up the beast's massive skull in my gun sight and patiently squeezed the trigger as its jaws opened in bloodthirst at a fleeing woman. An unexpected force bumped my shoulder from someone in the panicked crowd. I misfired into the sky above. Frank finished the job, knocking me down to the ground as he ran away. His eyes widened in fear.

The creature sank its teeth into the neck of a young woman and severed her throat. Blood gushed and splattered across the cafe's large window. It devoured the blood-soaked flesh torn from her. In a swift movement, the beast moved to the next patron and ripped a sizable chunk of flesh from her shoulder as it shredded her clothes.

Charles rushed in its direction, hopped onto a table, and recklessly charged toward it. I stood as he ran past me. The beast struck Charles to the ground and grabbed a man that stood nearby frozen in fear. It sank its teeth into his leg. Gun raised, I put the creature in my sights again. It turned and glared in my direction. Its teeth were prominent and covered in blood.

"What the hell are you doing here?" I mumbled, firing two shots, striking the creature in its head.

It fell to the ground as it wailed in pain. The body blistered and contorted as it transformed back into its human form. It twitched violently as its claws retracted, and fur pulled itself back into the strange man's flesh. A man not more than twenty-five years old lay dead and bleeding from his head in front of me.

"Oh, my God! What happened? It wasn't . . . I mean, *he* wasn't. It's . . . he's human?" Frank stuttered as he stood next to me.

Cries from the crowd sounded from those that didn't run at the sight of the creature.

"What are you doing back here? You literally knocked me down saving your own ass," I said.

"I've never seen anything like that before. What was it?" Frank asked, his eyes just as wide as before.

"Werewolf. I believed I killed all the ones here in town, or at least drove the last of them away years ago. I suppose I didn't, or a few of them made their way back," I answered as I re-holstered the backup gun.

Charles eventually made his way up from the ground and over to us. His eyes briefly closed as he shook his head. A blow to his pride, I'm sure.

"I guess that didn't go exactly as I planned it." Charles said. His hand rubbed the back of his neck, wincing.

He was lucky that thing didn't do more to him. I rushed over to the injured woman as she cried out. Blood soaked her torn yellow, green, and purple Mardi Gras themed shirt. I removed it to apply pressure to her wound. Her body wilted as she fell unconscious.

"She has a pulse. Charles, hold this in place and keep pressure on it," I said.

I ran over to the man with the bite in his leg. He cried out in agony as his hands clutched his wound.

"What's your name?" I asked, gently placing both hands on his uninjured leg.

"Chris. Chris Myers," he mumbled, grimaced in pain.

"Okay, Chris. Paramedics are on their way. I need you to take your shirt off and tie it around your leg right above your wound. They'll get you to the hospital. Just stay calm. You keep fighting, and I'll visit you in the hospital with an enormous slice of King Cake and some iced coffee." I turned my attention to Charles and his idiotic actions. "What the hell were you thinking attempting to take on a werewolf empty-handed? Where's your weapon?"

"I'm here on business, not hunting." His tone was condescending as he stared at the naked corpse bleeding on the ground with two bullet wounds in its head.

"That's not the hunter's code. The code is to always be prepared. But you know this already, don't you?" I rolled my eyes at the continued deceit that spilled from his mouth.

Frank stood nearby and swiped away any perceived dirt and dust that clung to his overpriced suit, starting with his pant leg, working his way to his suit coat, and adjusting his tie. "Charles, I believe this puts a bit of a hitch in our development plans. Was that what I think it was? I—I can't believe—"

"Mr. Lopez, please let me just explain," Charles pleaded as he followed Frank, who was walking away.

Police sirens that had previously whispered in the distance, grew closer as the vehicles came to a screeching halt in front of the cafe. They came from almost every direction. One-way signs disregarded.

As one vehicle came to a stop, and a familiar face stepped outside. The look of disgust on her face was just as apparent as the first time I met her. Captain Martel cut her eyes in my direction. Her top lip curled at the sight of me. I had seen other officers like her in the past. It didn't take long to turn them into what she had become. Bitter, ornery, and hellbent on making everyone around them miserable. As the saying goes, misery loves company. Her gun belt shifted on her waist as she walked feverishly toward me.

"Nola Maor, how did I know you would be involved in this somehow?"

"Your task force was a little too late to do anything about what happened. I was here luckily, or the loss of life would have been worse."

Captain Martel surveyed the immediate area around her and watched as the paramedics put both injured people on stretchers. The sparse crowd of people that remained wore textbook looks of shock on their faces. The faint sound of weeping could be heard in the distance.

"Ms. Maor, there are two dead bodies and multiple people injured. That's too much carnage. Two mauled with huge slices and bites ripped into them, one with her throat ripped out, and another with two bullet holes. This doesn't make much sense to me," Captain Martel said.

"It was a werewolf. I put it down after it attacked. I could only save the other two after I overcame the shock of what was happening. What took place is still a bit of a mystery to me. This one right here, with the two bullet wounds to the head, he's your werewolf," I said.

Captain Martel stared at me with her intense eyes, as if she could see right through me.

"Werewolf? In broad daylight? Do you take me for an idiot?"

"Well..."

"Captain Martel, we're getting conflicting statements from the witnesses that stuck around. Several aren't quite sure of what they saw, but we have quite a few statements saying they saw her with the gun in her hand. She pulled it from her ankle," the gangly built officer wearing blue cargo pants said.

"Process the scene and gather all the witness statements and info you can. We'll pass this off to the investigation's unit. Doesn't look like anything supernatural happened here," Captain Martel said with a grin.

"Are you kidding me? You can't be serious. What kind of half-ass investigator are you?"

"The kind that has enough probable cause to arrest you. Give me your weapon," Martel said.

I reached down and removed my backup gun from its holster. Ejecting the magazine, I removed the remaining bullet from the chamber and handed Captain Martel the unloaded handgun.

"This is a mistake," I said.

"It's not a mistake. It's been a long time coming. Turn around and put your hands behind your back. Nola Moar, you're under arrest for Second Degree Murder."

CHAPTER
SEVEN

"SOMETHING IS OUT THERE. I SAW SOMETHING MOVE."—JORDAN

Couples enjoyed the sunlit lake views from cozy benches, while families with children had fun rolling down the grassy hill at the well-known lakeside. When the sun set, the lakeside area became something unusual. An area veiled in night allowed some of the shadier people in the city to engage in unwholesome activities. Car sex and drug use were commonplace. It was a great location for friends to hangout and engage in other adult recreational activities when someone wanted to avoid being seen. In Alex's case, it was the perfect spot for him and his long-time friend, Gene, to toss back more than their fair share of beers. Having successfully avoided paying their bar tabs for years, Alex and Gene opted for post-work drinks by the lake. It was the next best thing. There was no bartender cutting them off after drinking an excessive amount and no loud annoying music selection that some young jerk at the jukebox. Alex and Gene sat at one of the picnic tables and bitched about their home lives and their jobs, all while they watched other degenerates come and go.

"Gene, I tell ya man, I don't know how much longer I can deal with this asshole boss of ours. Not sure if I have a bigger ballbuster at work or at home," Alex said.

Beads of sweat dotted his brow as his thick pink fingers gripped the beer bottle; Alex took another sip from the bottle as beer leaked from the corner of his mouth and into his unkempt ginger beard.

"Amen, brother. This is the only peace and quiet I get in a day. It never fails. As soon as I walk in the door at home, the wife will be there, waiting to nag me to death. Who needs that shit after dealing with management at that shithole of a job?" Gene said.

Alex and Gene had been friends since the day they both started at the warehouse uptown. Job opportunities in the city were scarce. When they were hired together, they quickly forged a bond. That was fifteen years ago. A couple of weddings and several children later, both Alex and Gene had settled into the role of bitter employee and uninvolved husbands that blamed the world for their problems. The problematic cliché was that alcohol was their refuge.

"Hey Alex, it's pretty dead out here. Usually there's one or two parked cars with couples inside that would give us a show. There's no peepshow tonight," Gene said, taking another gulp from his beer.

"Yeah, not sure what the hell is going on. Clear skies and cool air, you'd think there'd be a little more traffic. What the hell? A few more beers, and I'll call it a night," Alex said.

Laughter erupted as the two men bumped beer bottles. The

guttural wolf howl nearby caused the men to spring from the bench. Alex and Gene turned their heads and darted their eyes from side to side to investigate.

"What the hell was that?" Alex asked.

"I dunno. I know I've had a lot to drink, but that sounded a lot like a wolf," Gene replied.

In the distance, they noticed the headlights of an approaching car as it pulled into a parking spot and turned off its engine.

"Not sure what that noise was, but it looks like we're gonna get some entertainment after all," Alex said with a grin.

"Look, Alex, I know we've had a few, but you don't seem to be worried about whatever made that sound. Something doesn't feel right. It's been dead since we've been out here. Maybe we should just get the hell out of here," Gene said. His head swayed with apprehension back and forth as he observed his surroundings.

"Come on, Gene. It was probably just some—"

A beastly blur flashed past Alex. The massive figure pounced on top of Gene. The creature's huge canines violently chewed the flesh off of Gene's face. Blood poured from his gruesome fleshless skull. His blood soaked nasal cavity and set of teeth exposed. Alex was frozen in terror. Speechless, as his friend slumped lifelessly, the immense creature loomed over him. Alex inebriated body was slow to respond as he fell into the creature's grasp. Its massive claws gripped Alex's face. The beast swiftly ripped off his lower jaw. A crimson torrent spewed from the orifice as his hands reached in vain to clench his missing mandible. Alex's body fell limp next to Gene.

The night air stayed calm. The parked car and its passengers were undisturbed.

As I walked out of the cement monstrosity of Central Lock Up, the whispers of the sheriff's deputies behind me weren't so quiet. Guarding the gate, the women mumbled questions about my brief imprisonment and gossiped about how they could foresee my incarceration. My first instinct was to put messy little girls in their place. Better thoughts prevailed. The deputies weren't worth it. Besides, I would save that energy for Charles. He had it coming. I anxiously glanced down at my phone for the time.

Almost 9 p.m. Tammy's flight lands at ten o'clock. I need to get my car and get to the airport. I guess I'll give Jackson a call to come and pick me up.

As I looked at my phone, a familiar silver car pulled up beside me. Jordan's bright smile was the first sight as the passenger side window came down.

"Hey, good lookin'. You need a ride?" Jordan asked, leaning toward the passenger side door from the driver's seat.

"First, that was super cheesy. Second, perfect timing. How did you know they released me? I haven't had the chance to call anyone yet," I asked. I sat in the passenger seat of Jordan's car, which was much more comfortable than the unforgiving metal benches of that holding cell.

"Once I heard about the arrest, I started working on finding out what they had on you. Figured it was something bogus with Martel's daughter itching to hang you out to dry. It didn't take long to get you cleared with all the videos all over the internet. I'm surprised Jackson or Charles weren't already here to pick you up."

"I doubt Jackson knows anything about it. Charles, on the other hand . . . " My voice trailed off as I exhaled and leaned my head against the headrest. "What a day."

Jordan pulled away and drove a couple of miles into a less noisy area of the city. Only a couple of blocks away from his home, the lakefront was an area that allowed for fun family gatherings revolving around water play, barbecues, and music during the day and a calm atmosphere at night. The night sky hung over the largest lake in the state, offering the mirage of a boundless distance of water. A bright three-quarters moon was the sole source of light in the cloud blanketed sky.

I rolled down the window and allowed the subtle sound of the waves crashing into the concrete barrier to relax me as I took a few deep breaths. Jordan put his sizable hand on my thigh. I lifted my head and glared at him.

"You deserve better, Nola," Jordan said. His voice was gentle yet resonant and somehow a welcomed comfort.

His eyes had a softness to them. A kindness that radiated from deep within him. I didn't move his hand. I didn't want to move his hand. It was reassuring and felt natural. Jordan moved closer and kissed me. The softness of his lips was the only thing more intoxicating than his self-assurance. His other hand gently grasped around the small of my neck. I placed my hand on his strong chest, returning the passion emanating from his kiss. I could feel the quickened pace of his heartbeat. It excited me.

With the swing of my leg, I hopped over and sat in Jordan's lap, removing my blouse above my head. My bra quickly followed. Jordan shed his shirt, and our naked bodies made contact. The heat from his body was enthralling. He gently but firmly pushed me away after grabbing my shoulders.

"Are you sure?" he asked.

"Well, you came here to give me a ride. Don't stop now," I said with a smile, a nervous attempt to break the tension. Jordan smiled in return.

I could feel his desire for me and somehow removed my pants quicker than I could remember. Straddling his lap, I felt the grip of his large hands pressed against my back. It was almost overwhelming. It was something I needed.

That didn't go how Jordan planned. Someday, he knew he would need to admit his feelings to Nola. To sway her toward him, maybe a candlelit dinner in an upscale restaurant, adorned with flowers and passionate arguments, would do the trick. Jordan glanced over at Nola and noticed the smile on her face as they both maneuvered inside the car and buckled their pants. Jordan couldn't help but smile as well.

"So, should we—"

"We won't talk about this right now. Tammy should be landing any minute, and we need to get to the airport," Nola said, interrupting Jordan.

"Umm . . . sure. If that's how you want to handle it, we can talk about it—" Jordan paused as he looked out the rearview mirror. His brow curled as he turned his head to peer out the driver's side window as he let it down. "Nola, I—"

"Jordan, I said I don't want to address it now," Nola again interrupted. Her tone dripped with frustration.

Jordan turned to her and pressed his index finger over his mouth with wide eyes to silence Nola. He leaned slightly toward the window to listen to the subtle sounds of the night. The tiny hairs on his arm stood as his heart thumped faster.

"Something is out there. I saw something move," Jordan said. He pulled his handgun from under the driver's seat.

"What did you see?" Nola asked.

"I'm not sure, but I think we're being hunted. Grab Corbin," Jordan replied.

"Damn it. I put Corbin in the trunk when you picked me up. The police still have my backup gun locked up in evidence."

Jordan turned and pointed to a latch attached to the back seat of the car. "You can get to the trunk from inside. Just crawl back there and pull the latch," Jordan whispered.

A nearby howl pierced the silence of the night. His eyes darted from the rearview mirror to the side mirror. A shadowy blur circled the car. Panicked, Jordan reached for the car door handle. The driver's side window of the car shattered.

Nola desperately lunged to the back seat to reach the latch for Corbin. Shards of glass sliced into her arm. The growls of the creature were closer. The rear passenger side window shattered. Nola screamed and ducked onto the back seat. The werewolf's sharp claws shattered the back windshield as it dove inside. Its massive body collided with the front seats. Nola quickly slid out of the broken passenger side window away from the werewolf. The creature swiped at the back of Jordan's head as he ducked away from the glass.

Jordan leaped from the car to the ground. The werewolf's claws tore through the interior. Jordan and Nola watched as clouds of cotton from the car seats were ripped and tossed into the air.

The beast thrusted its head out of the back window. Its claws reached out from within the vehicle and gripped each side of the car door. It bared its chattering teeth at Jordan and Nola. Its eyes filled with bloodthirst. Jordan raised his gun and fired a couple of shots. The silver bullets struck the werewolf in the neck and chest. The squeal of the beast carried in the night air. Blood spattered upon the upholstery. The body of the werewolf twisted and contorted violently as it changed back into human form in the backseat of Jordan's car.

"Are you kidding me? Twice in one day. How many of them are there?" Nola said. She placed her hands on her knees, bent over as she attempted to catch her breath.

Jordan tucked the gun back into the inner belt of his waistline. "I don't know. Definitely enough for a pack. Strangely, I think that thing was targeting me," Jordan said.

"Why would you think that?" Nola asked.

"Just my instincts. It may have been tracking me most of the night. When it got inside, it only took a swipe at me, not you," Jordan replied.

"That's a leap, Jordan. We don't know what the hell is going on. I will admit, whatever is going on is escalating. Let's just keep everything that happened tonight between us until we can figure things out," Nola said. Her eyes softened as she pleaded with him.

Jordan hesitated. His mouth dangled open, as he desperately wanted to convince Nola otherwise. He reached into his pocket and handed her another set of keys. Nola was right.

Now wasn't the time or place to talk this through. Not without everyone else.

"Nola, I'm not sure if that's the right move. There better be a method to your madness. If not, I'll tell Jackson we were attacked tonight. I trust my instincts, and he deserves to know. For now, take these keys and get to my house. It's a few blocks away. I have another car you can use to pick up Tammy. I'll catch up with you guys later. The car needs my attention."

CHAPTER
EIGHT

"NO LIES, CHARLES. RIGHT NOW, MY EYES ARE WIDE OPEN. I SEE YOU." — NOLA

Jackson leaned back with his right fist to summon as much force as he could as he lunged forward, furious and consumed by the thought of dislocating Charles' lower jaw and knocking a significant number of teeth out of his mouth. In that moment, Jackson forgot all the fight training he had spent years perfecting. Charles slightly leaned his muscular frame away from Jackson's misguided punch, which caused Jackson to lose balance. Charles extended his arm; his powerful biceps wrangled Jackson's body around the neck. His arms wrapped tight around his head and neck in the wrestler's sleeper hold as Charles lifted Jackson off the ground. As his feet dangled, Charles squeezed his hold a little more, restricting Jackson's oxygen as he struggled to reach the ground.

"Kid, I love you. Hell, I've liked you from the moment I met you in Dalyville. I know what you've been through. I was there. Since me and your aunt have been together, I tried to be like a father figure in your life. It's something I never had."

Panicked, Jackson slapped at Charles' arms as he struggled

to breathe. Jackson kicked his legs back; his heels struck Charles shins. No effect.

"With that said, one piece of advice. Stay in your lane. Don't fuck with me," Charles whispered. His breath gently brushed against Jackson's ear.

The tone of his voice unmistakably committed to whatever ideas presented themselves in his thoughts. Jackson grabbed Charles' arms as he tried to free himself up, gasping for air, still in a bit of shock at Charles' actions. He knew he was a former soldier. A trained hunter. Yet, Charles had always been in control. Jackson thought he had the training to deal with someone like him after so much time in the streets hunting all manner of things. Charles was more formidable than he thought, and if Jackson was honest, he didn't expect this type of reaction. Jackson's eyes caught the mirror in front of him. He saw the look of fear and panic on his face before his sight became blurry. Charles released his hold on Jackson. He fell to the floor, hand on his chest as he inhaled deeply, trying to replenish his lungs with oxygen.

"Why in the hell did you let the cops take her? Did you even bother to vouch as a witness when they showed up? You never step up when she needs you! Let me guess . . . money was on your mind?" Jackson stood as he maneuvered his head side to side to relieve the pain in his neck. His hand clutched on the black rubber handle of the Guardian affixed to his belt.

"Easy, kid. There's no need for that. I was lost in what I was chasing. I would never let anything happen to Nola. My love for her is immeasurable. I just wish I knew her sooner. Maybe things would be different," Charles responded.

As Charles continued his rather shaky explanation, the front door of Jackson's home opened. Nola and Tammy entered with only Tammy offering a smile. Jackson and Charles stood in the middle of the living room, saturated with tension. A smile slowly crept upon the face of Jackson as he recognized the strawberry-colored cheeks of his longtime friend. The obvious contrast was the look of pure anger and vitriol that emanated from Nola's eyes as she picked up on the apparent issue that happened only moments before she walked into the room.

"What the hell?! What's going on with you? You let them take me. You said nothing, and you did nothing," I fumed.

"I went after Frank. There were enough witnesses, and I was certain they couldn't hold you on anything. I was right in my assumption, correct?" Charles continued before I could reply. "They let you out, and you still had time to go and get Tammy from the airport. I'm sorry, but Frank is our ticket out of this life. I needed to talk him down and keep him from panicking."

"You ran behind some old ass investor promising stacks of cash, instead of standing by my side? Do you have any idea what I've been through today?" The palm of my hand seared with pain from the ferocity in which I clenched my fist tightly, pressing my nails into my flesh. "You knew how unhinged that bitch captain was, and her plans to do what she could to lock me up for good. You did nothing!" A heat flushed my skin as if I stood next to a blazing fire. "You were right, though. Some of the patrons who were there caught it all with their cell phone cameras and brought it to the police department's leadership. They had to let me go. Good thing Jordan was already at lockup checking on me, thanks to a call from one of his contacts advising him of my release. He gave me a ride," I said with a crooked smile.

Charles squinted. "It figures he'd be standing around waiting to play the hero. You know he wants to sleep with you, right?" Charles said. He moved a step back away from me.

"I don't care what he wants. He was there for me. Then I walked in here, and there was clearly something about to go down between you and Jackson. Do you want to talk about that, or do you want to talk about how you've been lying to me about going out of town on business?"

"Nola, I—I can explain." Charles interrupted.

"You seem to say that a lot these days," I said, waving him away with my hand.

"Don't wave your hand at me like I'm some child you're brushing aside. I deserve more respect from you. You damn right I went behind the money. Hell, my money is the reason we can afford all the silver we need to do the hunting we need to do."

"So now you're lying to me and throwing your money in my face? Who are you? What the hell is wrong with you, Charles?" I asked, shaking my head in disbelief.

"Nola, I didn't mean to—"

"No more lies, Charles. Right now, my eyes are wide open. I see you." Jackson and Tammy put off the warm welcome and turned their attention toward me and Charles.

I didn't want to do this in front of Jackson, but I also didn't want to give Charles more time to come up with any creative lies.

"About a year ago, a real estate developer by the name of Frank Lopez contacted me about a major project here in the city. He was considering a partnership with the firm for major redevelopment and reallocation of land and salvageable structures for housing, schools, and businesses. He chose the firm because he had done business with it in the past, and it was obscenely profitable. The new venture was an ambitious project that would have brought my company and possibly our livelihood up a couple of levels. The plan reminded me of what my mother had planned for Dalyville, except on a much larger scale."

"Possibly?" I interjected.

"Yes, possibly. We aren't married, remember? You've made sure of that. You've deliberately kept me at arm's length. Guarded every step of the way. It's held us back. You know it, and I know it. We just don't talk about it."

The corner of Charles' mouth lifted ever so slightly. Barely noticeable if someone wasn't paying attention. I was paying attention. He wanted to get that off his chest for a while.

"What does that have to do with—"

"I'm getting there." Charles glared at me and squared his shoulders in my direction.

"Things were going fine. Business was going well, and Frank and I had developed plans for thirty square blocks in different parts of the city. Then something set off some alarms within me. He started asking about you, Nola," Charles said.

"Excuse me? How does he know me? We just met."

"He didn't speak of you by name. But he stated he was curious about the mysterious supernatural hunter of New

Orleans he heard so much about. In getting to know our common interests, we discovered we were both into the occult. Red flag, I know. The world revealed these things, but people remain asleep or unconcerned. On top of that, we like to keep a low profile. So, when he started steering our conversations to the occult, I got a little suspicious. Frank was a little too aggressive in asking his questions. Sometimes our conversations felt more like an interrogation to get information than simple words between colleagues."

Tammy and Jackson moved over to the couch. Their brief joyous reunion was no longer at the forefront. Tammy squinted as she listened to Charles convey his concerns.

"Charles, I don't understand. Why didn't you tell me about your concerns? I've never met Frank in person during this business in New York. I've seen him mentioned in correspondence, but—," Tammy said before the faint sound of a hum interrupted.

The front right pocket of my jeans vibrated as I veered my eyes away from Tammy and back toward Charles, awaiting his response. No indication he was lying, but he was omitting something. I squeezed the buttons on the side of the phone through my pocket to silence its annoyance.

"I have a better question. Why would he be asking probing questions about me to you? Why would he think you're the Subject Matter Expert on all things Nola Maor?" I asked, as I ensured his eyes didn't veer away.

"I may have mentioned we were dating after he told me he was a fan of the occult. I didn't think much of it at the time. It seemed like a good way to bolster our newly established business connection."

"Exactly how much did you share about us?" I asked. My hands quivered. I crossed my arms to hide them.

"A few things. Our potential marriage, Jackson, and the death of your parents and sister."

Red was the primary color I saw surrounding me as I approached Charles and struck him across the face. I moved swiftly and swung with all the power I had with my right hand. Charles' head only slightly moved at the punch. It felt as though I hit a brick wall. A small trickle of blood flowed from the corner of his mouth. He dabbed it away with the back of his hand. Charles glared back at me. It lingered. His eyes were empty, as if everything inside of him momentarily disappeared. He blinked rapidly as his eyes filled with tears.

"Son of a bitch! What gives you the right to share that with some stranger?"

"Nothing, baby. I'm sorry, but you need to hear the rest." Charles moved further across the room, away from me, rubbing the side of his face. "The questions didn't sit right with me and since I regretted answering them anyway, I decided to look a little deeper into him. Past the financial records and S.E.C. filings. So, I followed Frank. It didn't take long. The first night I followed his taxi ride, I noticed I wasn't the only one following him. There was a lycanthrope trailing him. It jumped from roof to roof to keep pace with the taxi. It was the first one I'd seen in New Orleans," Charles said.

"Christ! Do you think it was trying to kill him?" I asked.

"Not sure. He made it into the hotel lobby before it could make a move without being seen. If that's what it wanted."

"That doesn't make any sense. Werewolves aren't usually that tactical. They're hunters, but if it wants a meal, it'll take it regardless of the risk. I'm sure it could have gotten to him and ripped that cab apart if it wanted to," Jackson said. He took a couple of steps toward Charles.

"And today he happens to be there when one attacks in broad daylight?" I asked.

"What!?" Tammy asked with startled eyes.

"Yeah, first time I had ever heard or seen such a thing. And my hero here chased Frank after I put it down, instead of helping me secure the situation. It looks like they had a particular interest in him for some reason. Werewolves are back in this city. I guess my warning to stay out didn't reach enough of them," I said.

"Auntie, there hasn't been any news coverage on mutilated bodies. Nothing to indicate there were any here." Jackson walked over to the couch and plopped down. "Except I heard one howl the other night when I followed Charles. There was definitely one in the abandoned amusement park," Jackson said.

"I've been hunting them. It's why I've been lying about leaving town for the past month or so. I knew if there was one, there were more," Charles added.

"You've been hunting them . . . alone?" I asked.

"Your parents, Nola . . . What happened to your parents still affects you. You're still angry, and your PTSD struggles don't help. Hunting these things might make you reckless. I was trying to protect you."

Charles hesitated as he stepped closer to me. I held the palm of my hand out as a means of dissuasion.

"I don't know what your reasoning is to hunt these things on your own, but you weren't protecting me. You were protecting yourself," I said, turning my body away from Charles and toward Jackson and Tammy. "Jackson, there was one mutilated body that I'm aware of. It's hard to say how many more there were with the way that task force operates holding back information. I can't determine if these murders with the missing hearts are connected. It's not a werewolf's M.O."

I walked to the cherry wood cabinet in the far corner of the room, retrieved the keys in my pocket, and unlocked it. The smell of gun oil and wood polish made for a unique and pleasing combination. I retrieved the small black nylon bag, which hung on a hook on the right interior door.

"Jackson, call Chloe. Get her over here if she's available. You guys hit the books and the computer and find out as much as you can about Frank Lopez, and I mean everything."

"You got it," Jackson replied.

"Tammy, you said you've spoken with Mr. Lopez before. I'm sure since Charles is in business with him, you know some of his business dealings and can probably help Jackson with some insight."

"No problem, Nola," Tammy replied.

"Charles, you can leave. You've chosen to work alone. Don't let us get in your way."

The phone in my pocket vibrated again, violently shaking against my leg. I again sent it to voicemail.

"Auntie, where are you going?" Jackson asked.

I hurriedly slipped on my shoulder gun holster and strapped Corbin in tightly, inspecting it again to make sure there were no issues like before. A black jacket concealed it as I glanced at the clock on the wall that read a few minutes after midnight. The day had been eventful.

"There's some unfinished business from today's attack that needs my attention. I'll be back shortly."

CHAPTER NINE

"HOW DID IT FEEL?" — THE COLLECTOR

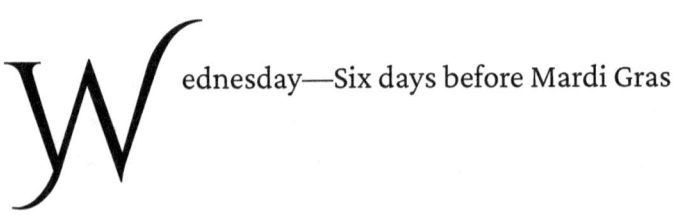

Wednesday—Six days before Mardi Gras

HOSPITALS ALWAYS SMELLED of rubbing alcohol and bleach, which I found to be the worst part of them. Following Goliath's near-fatal attack, my hospital stay was marked by continuous pain and the ever-present threat of vomiting every hour. The nausea, mostly because of crushing anxiety and that potent scent wasn't a memory I hurried to revisit. Jackson or Charles had to drag me into hospitals kicking and screaming for anything longer than a simple doctor's visit.

One thing I could count on was that New Orleans' number one trauma hospital would be active even at 1 a.m. on a Wednesday. The city didn't sleep, and neither did its crime. The rush of scrub garbed nurses and white coat doctors bouncing from one severely afflicted trauma patient to the next made it relatively easy to walk into the emergency room and sneak my way into the intensive care unit. A quick change into my own set of scrubs helped me blend in with ease.

The ICU, on the other hand, was almost a ghost town at this time of night, just like any other hospital. Most of the patient's doors were closed, but the blinds to the windows remained up for a quick and easy check-in by the staff. Not surprisingly, the active nurses on the floor were sparse. Overnight shifts were all the same; lots of people on the clock and hiding in various places, trying to sneak in a nap, hide from work, or engage in other naughty activities. Only a few yards from the nurse's desk, I peered into the window of the darkened room to my left as I approached.

The pale woman lying in bed rested peacefully, as the IV tubes attached pulled at her arms. Electrodes clung to her chest, monitoring vitals. She could have passed as someone sleeping soundly, had it not been for the bandages covering part of her neck and shoulder.

I crept inside and kept a firm grip on the door handle while closing the door and then shutting the blinds. The aroma of the rubbing alcohol seemed stronger inside the room. My stomach twisted with nausea and tension. I quietly cleared my throat to convince the late dinner I scarfed down twenty minutes ago not to revisit me. I stood next to the bed and looked down at her soft features. She might have sensed my presences as her eyes opened and cut in my direction. I returned a tight-lipped smile in sympathy.

"I know you," her dry voice cracked as she widened her eyes. "You saved my life again."

"Shhh. Rest. Don't get yourself worked up," I replied. I

grabbed the handle of the Styrofoam container and the cup near her, poured some water, and handed it to her. I sat on the edge of the bed next to her and held her hand.

Wincing, she struggled to raise the cup to her mouth, but she was still able to sip. Her shoulders slumped in relief as she closed her eyes momentarily.

"Thank you." She managed a crooked smile. "I know who you are. Even when I was lying on the ground bleeding after that thing bit me, I recognized your face. I'm a bit of a fan. I never thought I would get the chance to meet you, Nola." Her smile was a little more prominent as she wiggled her body to sit up straight.

A grin crept upon my face as she became lively, yet grimaced in pain.

"What do you mean, I saved your life again?"

"It was about ten years ago. Before I got married and had a son. I was out partying with two of my girlfriends. We got a little tipsy and wandered onto a dark street near the levy wall in the Bywater area. We knew about Goliath and all that had happened, but we didn't care." She laughed as she reflected on her memories, before her facial expression went blank. She stared at the wall as she recalled the horrors.

"We weren't the best decision makers at that age. There was partying to do, so we didn't care much. Just our luck, a vampire attacked us and killed my friends." Her eyes welled as she spoke. "It ripped their throats open. Blood went . . . everywhere. Oh my God, there was so much red. My friend's blood sprayed all over my face. It covered my eyes and spilled into my mouth. I can still feel the warmth against my skin, the metallic taste of it." She wiped the tears away and continued, "You came out of nowhere and killed it right before it took my life. Ever since then, I kept a close eye on everything involved with the occult. Learned as much as I could about it and about you. I owe my life to you," she said, her eyes continued to well with tears.

"I remember that night. All night, I tracked that parasite. I'm sorry I didn't get there in time to help your friends." I squeezed her hand firmly to comfort her. "Do you know what happened today? Did anyone tell you?"

She again winced in pain, reaching for her heavily bandaged left side as she sat up, a little firmer. "I know what I saw. I couldn't believe what I was looking at. To see one in person was something I never expected. I saw it running toward us and pretty much froze. I couldn't make a sound and I couldn't get my legs to work. Before I knew it, it was ripping into me," she said.

"A werewolf," I replied.

"Yes. I can still feel its teeth gnawing at my flesh. My blood splattered into my eyes and blurred my vision. Just like that night ten years ago. The only thing I could hear was its low-pitched growl. Then I heard gunshots, and I saw your face. I've never felt so relieved. I knew I would be fine, but I don't remember much after that," she said, staring at me with a smile and a look of gratitude in her eyes. Tears continued to fall as her breathing became labored. The monitors attached to her started beeping rapidly.

I dropped to the floor and slipped under the bed as the door flung open. Blue scrubs and white shoes approached the bed.

"Are you okay?" the nurse asked.

"I'm fine. Just had a nightmare. I guess I was kind of reliving what happened in my sleep. It got me worked up," the patient responded.

The alerts from the monitor quieted.

I lay silently on the cold floor as the nurse maneuvered around the bed and checked her vitals. The smell of the cleaning solution used on the tile floor crept into my nose, nauseating me. I needed the nurse to leave before I vomited all over the nice, clean tile.

"Okay, your vitals seem fine. Would you like anything to help you get back to sleep?" the nurse asked.

"No. I think I'll be okay. Just need to clear my head a bit."

"Rest up. Make sure you remember to click that little button next to you if you feel any discomfort," the nurse said.

The covers shifted as she left the room.

"That wasn't fun," I said, sliding out from under the bed and dusting myself off as I stood. "Thanks for covering for me."

A look of sorrow crossed the patient's face and her eyes watered as she turned her head to look at me.

"I'm not going to be fine, am I?" Her voice trembled.

"What's your name, sweetheart?" I asked. I squeezed her hand a little tighter.

"J-Janice," she stuttered.

My throat swelled with emotion at the sound of the name that stumbled from her mouth. With my back to her, I rushed to the corner of the hospital room, shaking what felt like blood-drenched hands.

"Are you okay?" Janice asked.

A couple of deep breaths allowed me to gather myself and walk back towards the bed and hold her hand. "Janice, that's a beautiful name. Someone I loved very much had that name. How are you feeling?"

"Lots of pain, but strong. I feel really... strong."

"T-that's great to hear," I said somberly. Eyes lingering on Janice's wound, I squeezed her hand tighter.

Janice widened her eyes as if some crucial missing detail had just occurred to her.

"Please. Please don't. I have a family. I have a son and a husband. Besides, I've read all about this. A bite doesn't automatically mean you'll change. It doesn't mean—"

"Janice, you shouldn't feel strong only a few hours after an attack and surgery. You probably shouldn't even be conscious. My reason for being here is your family. I know what it's like. I've experienced the pain of losing a loved one. You don't want to be responsible for that." My hand slipped behind me and gripped the handle of the silver blade tucked in my waistband.

"Let's just give it some more time. It's possible—"

Janice's words fell silent as I plunged the silver blade of my serrated hunting knife into the base of her skull. Her body fell limp. Her eyes closed as blood poured from her temple and soaked into the pillow. Tears fell from my eyes as I released her hand and unplugged the monitor attached to her.

"Goodnight, Janice."

As I slid the knife back into its holster, my thigh vibrated. I quickly wiped the tears from my eyes and reached into my pocket to retrieve the cell phone. I couldn't take my eyes off Janice. Her lifeless eyes were still open.

My God, what have I done?

Nauseated at the thought of what I did, I managed to glance down at the phone. The sight of his name on my screen caused me to bite down on my bottom lip to suppress the scream that erupted inside me. With each step, the phone vibrated incessantly. 'The Collector' brightly displayed on the screen. The beat of my heart quickened, and I wiped the beaded moisture from my brow as I moved back to the corner of the room and away from Janice's body. Answering that phone was the last thing I wanted to do. I needed a moment to gather myself, but the persistent shaking of the phone pushed me to answer.

"What do you want?" I asked, pinching the bridge of my nose with my thumb and index finger, eyes closed in frustration.

"How did it feel?" the familiar voice on the other end replied.

"Excuse me? What in the hell are you talking about?"

"I know where you are, and I know what you're doing. You killed that poor woman before her change. She had a powerful and amazing life ahead of her. You took that from her. Your selfish and self-righteous ideology took that woman from her family. This is a perfect example of why you're on the wrong side of everything. Your parents deserved what happened to them, and you deserve what's coming to you. Don't let me interrupt you. Isn't there one more person you need to murder?"

The phone clicked, and the call ended abruptly.

I detested every word he said. The words hurt me even more severely than I anticipated. Deep breaths, taken again and again, steadied my hands. The Collector was right. There was another person bitten in this hospital I needed to kill.

CHAPTER
TEN
"I'VE SEEN ONE LIKE THAT BEFORE." — NOLA

"This isn't enough! He deserves so much more. I've failed this kid at every turn."

"Nola, calm down. This is great. Jackson will love this. He loves you and I'm sure he'll appreciate anything you do for him," Tammy said. She continued to hang the black balloons along the trim of the ceiling. Jordan worked toward Tammy from the other end as I walked up behind him.

"Hey, it was a long day yesterday, and I didn't get the chance to check in with you. Thanks for everything last night. Were you able to take care of our little problem?" I whispered.

"All taken care of, Nola. I disposed of both the car and the body. I reported the car as stolen, and no one will find that body. He'll end up as a missing person's report eventually, if he has any family left. Kinda sad when you think about it," Jordan replied. He glanced toward Tammy to ensure she didn't hear him.

"Did you remember to get his fingerprints so we can keep an eye on any investigations where his name pops up?"

"Nola, I got this. I know the job. Relax and maybe don't talk so loudly," Jordan said.

"Don't worry. Tammy has been a part of the family since Dalyville. Even if she heard us, she knows how things go. Besides, I planned on coming clean to everyone about it all soon."

Tammy was one of the few people I felt comfortable opening up to outside of Charles. She understood the persistent pain and struggles that plagued me. The night terrors, crippling anxiety, along with the grief from the loss of both parents and a sibling, had been an overbearing hurdle. I couldn't always lay those issues in Charles' lap. He lost the only parent he had ever known, and that same woman was a mentor to Tammy. She was the listener I needed. I'm sure Jackson has leaned on her as well, in light of how close they had grown over the years.

Charles, on the other hand, didn't talk much about it. He listened, but I could tell when I tried to open up, he would rather move past it all. I saw what inner turmoil did to a person. I wouldn't let it consume me or Jackson. That was why everything had to be perfect for Jackson's party. The kid had a lifetime ahead of him, and I wanted him to be normal. Well, as normal as this lifestyle allowed.

Everything was in place. The cake. The balloons. The gifts. Ice cream and chocolate syrup. All ready to go. Jackson's relentless sweet tooth would be well-satisfied.

I wasn't sure how Jackson had fallen in love with horror movies. You would think that hunting these things was enough, but he still gots a thrill from it all. Jackson loved the campy stuff. Tammy suggested cardboard cutouts of all the horror classics. Dracula, Frankenstein, The Wolfman, and of course, The Creature from the Black Lagoon were all present and ready for pictures with the guests. Tammy placed the candles in the cake and slapped her hands together to symbolize all the tasks were completed.

"Sweets as far as the eye can see. Jackson is going to love you two for this. Given everything you've been through together, you're lucky to have each other," Jordan said. Jordan stood there and gazed at me with a crooked grin. His stance was firm.

You could tell he was a former cop, and he knew how to handle himself. He staggered his feet, shoulder-width apart, and clasped his large hands together, always above his waist and ready to move at a moment's notice. Jordan's demeanor had oozed confidence since the day I met him. The thought of those hands gripping the flesh of my bare back gave me goosebumps. I let out a sharp exhale as I veered my gaze away from him to shake the memory.

"Done! Chloe texted me. They should walk in any minute. She mentioned the party was perfect timing after midterm exams just finished up." Tammy walked over and placed her hand on my back and gently rubbed. "Everything will be fine. Although, I tried to call and text Charles. He didn't respond."

"I'm not surprised. He's been chasing that developer around with ideas of becoming wealthier, not to mention his doubts about him. He's been distracted lately, and I haven't been able to get through to him. Now the lying. He better not screw this up. I need this to work out. Things are getting unpredictable with the daylight attack that happened yesterday, the unusual deaths in the city, and these weird phone calls I've been getting. Something is brewing. As a matter of fact, I think it's all about to boil over," I said.

"What weird phone calls?" Tammy asked.

The front door opened. Jackson walked in smiling and carrying an overstuffed backpack, with Chloe on his arm. Jackson walked with the confidence of a man who could conquer every obstacle in his path. His smile was still as bright as the day I saw him as that gangly teenager back in Dalyville. The way Jackson carried himself often put me at ease. Still, things happened even to the strongest of us. It would only take one bad day for things to go terribly wrong. That was the day that had me worried. Today, I watched him laugh as he looked around the room and noticed the cheesy decor for his party. Definitely the reaction I hoped for.

"So, no one is gonna yell, 'Surprise?'" Jackson yelled as loud as he could with one hand placed on the side of his mouth.

Chloe laughed and playfully slapped Jackson on the shoulder. "You know this isn't a surprise party, jerk," Chloe said, pulling the backpack from his shoulders and tossing it aside. "Excuse him please, Nola. He insists on being a clown sometimes."

Chloe's eyes brightened when she spoke about Jackson. Filled with a nascent love that I had seen with others in my early years, but one I never experienced. Her smiled widened when Jackson placed a gentle kiss upon her cheek. Chloe's face became crimson like a cherry.

"Don't I know it," I replied.

"Happy birthday, Jackson. There will be many more happy ones ahead. I love you." I grabbed ahold of his arm, yanked him closer, and wrapped my arms around him as tight as I could.

"Easy. Easy there, Auntie. Do you know how strong you are? I've seen you do push-ups," Jackson replied, wrapping his arms around me. His body shook with laughter.

"Boy, hush!"

"Seriously, thank you, Aunt Nola. It's been a rough few years for both of us. I appreciate all of this. Without you and Tammy, I'm not certain how I would have survived. I love you too." Jackson pulled back and gave me his signature smile.

He then wrapped his arms around Tammy and picked her up off her feet, squeezing her tightly. "I love you too, little Tammy!" He growled as he gently spun her around.

Her legs stiffened at the suffocating bear hug. "Jackson, if you don't put me down, I'm going to kick you in the balls," Tammy yelled, her brow furrowed.

The room erupted in laughter at the deepened voice that spilled from Tammy and her tiny frame. Jackson put her down immediately.

"Tammy, small but deadly. Just like dynamite." Jackson continued to laugh.

Tammy threw a few playful punches at Jackson's shoulder. Her once pale face was now bloodred with embarrassment.

Jackson held out his arm to shake Jordan's hand. "Jordan, thank you for coming. I'm glad you're here. I'm sure Aunt Nola is glad as well. Aren't you, Aunt Nola?" Jackson's lips tucked inward with a smirk.

I glared at him. "I see you are still working your way to that kick in the balls?" I said.

Jackson threw his hands in the air with a smirk, maybe realizing he went a little too far.

"No, ma'am. I don't want any trouble."

Jordan turned his head away from me, probably from embarrassment.

"Happy birthday, Jackson. You're an exceptional young man and a good friend," Jordan replied.

Jackson glanced over at the brightly colored purple and red Dracula themed cake on the table. He rubbed his hands together and licked his lips as he stared down at it.

"Can we cut this now?" Jackson asked.

"No food, huh? Straight to the dessert?" I asked.

Jackson hunched his shoulders in reply. Those tucked lips and smirk were present once again.

"Wait, isn't someone missing?" Jackson turned his head back and forth and scanned the living room.

I clenched my jaw. "Jackson, I'm sorry. We tried to reach Charles all day, but—"

"Charles? I don't care where he is. I'm talking about Mrs. Bradley. She can probably hear everything happening in here. I'm sure she could use the company. She doesn't have anyone," Jackson answered.

"Damn it! Jackson, I'm sorry I forgot. I told her about the party, but I--"

The front door opening interrupted me.

Charles' untimely appearance sent my heart racing, anger coursing through me. Everyone in the room turned their focus in his direction. Charles closed the door behind him without a single sign of regret in his body language.

"Sorry I'm late. I had some business I needed to attend to," Charles said.

"You could have stayed where you were. You gotta take care of what's important to you, right?" The once bright smile on Jackson's face was gone as he bared his teeth in a vitriolic way.

"Look, you little . . . " Charles started. "Again, I'm sorry. Time got away from me." He squinted, yet his eyes softened when he veered in my direction.

"Finish it," I said, as my pulse quickened.

"What?" Charles asked.

"Finish what you were about to say to Jackson. I want to hear what you wanted to say." I took a couple of steps closer to Charles.

"Let's just agree Charles is an asshole for being late and move on. I think we need to focus on getting Mrs. Bradley over here and coming up with a damn good excuse on why there's a late invite," Chloe interjected. "That woman can be a handful."

I could appreciate Chloe trying to keep the peace, but I wasn't letting Charles off the hook that easily. The uncomfortable silence and tension in the atmosphere lasted only a few brief moments. A high-pitched squeal and crashing sound of shattering glass cut through the silence. I widened my eyes as I made my way to the window that faced Mrs. Bradley's house.

"What in the hell was that?" Jordan whispered.

I placed my finger on top of my lips, glaring in Jordan's direction. Tilting my head closer to the window, I glanced behind the curtain into the darkness.

"I can't see anything, and I don't hear anything now. I need to go over and check on Mrs. Bradley. Maybe she had some sort of accident. Jackson, grab Corbin from the top of the fridge. You and Jordan come with me, just in case."

Jackson handed me Corbin as we made our way to the front door. Charles darted his eyes at me. His jawline tensed with anger.

"It takes three hunters to check in on an old lady? She could have fallen, and we're wasting time over here planning for some sort of attack. Don't you guys think this is a little ridiculous?"

The smug look on Charles's face pissed me off and put him a little deeper in the doghouse. Now was not the time.

"Just in case it's not a fall, Charles, stay here with Tammy and Chloe. They might need you. Can you manage that?" I asked.

The piercing sound of a howl filled the air as we stepped outside. Jackson and I stepped out into the well-lit neighborhood. The buzz of the electricity coursing through the nearby lamp post was the only prevalent sound in the still air of the night.

A quick glance to the left and right revealed nothing but the familiar surroundings I saw daily. The Robertson's pink swing set for their daughter, Jenny, which sat in their front yard. Old man Connor's rusted out '67 Caddy still sitting on cinder blocks in his driveway. He's been trying to restore that hunk of junk for eight years. As of late, Mrs. Bradley's gaudy Mardi Gras decorations had become bolder each year. This year had to be a personal record for her when it came to light decor. Her shotgun house stuck out like a sore thumb with blinking of the purple and green lights.

Jackson and I stood in the street and scanned the stillness of the night. The footsteps of everyone who should have been inside the house broke the silence as they appeared on the front porch. Their reckless behavior wasn't an endearing trait at the moment. The rapid taps of Jackson's hand on my shoulder compounded my annoyance. The once subtle squeak of Mrs. Bradley's screen door cut through the air like a high-pitched scream. Jackson's widened eyes and fearful stare at Mrs. Bradley's house forced me to look over my shoulder.

"Aunt Nola, l-look at the size of that t-thing," Jackson stammered over his words. Fear drenched his voice.

A massive beast stomped out of the front door of Mrs. Bradley's home. For its size, it was quite nimble. Coarse gray hair covered its body, and its eyes glowed a burning flame red. Its massive claws wrapped around the head of a body, dragging the woman behind it. Its claws wrapped around Mrs. Bradley's head as she grasped the lycanthrope's fur covered arm. Her squeal-like screams echoed in the night as she kicked in terror. It dragged her down the stairs of the porch and into the street. The violent thumping in my chest reverberated in my ears as I struggled to catch my breath. This beast wasn't like the one that attacked at the coffee shop. It was different. Not just the size of it, but its glowing red pupils and enlarged canine teeth triggered a visceral fear within me. It was familiar. Everything about it was familiar.

It lifted Mrs. Bradley, its claws still wrapped around her fragile head. Mrs. Bradley's scream pulled the rest of the neighbors out of their homes, drawn by the commotion.

"Nola!" Jordan yelled, his brow curled, nodding his head toward the creature.

Corbin in hand, I raised my arm and pulled the trigger. The bullets ripped through the creature's flesh. Blood trickled down its grayish fur. The creature was unaffected and didn't move. Its unnatural body pushed the spent silver bullets from its powerful chest and abdomen. The bullets bounced on the concrete like coins that fell from a purse. The werewolf glared at me and snarled, baring saliva between moistened teeth. It was as if it was taunting me. With its other hand, it raised its index finger near its head. Its motion waved back and forth as if it was telling me no. It moved its sharpened nail toward Mrs. Bradley. Her screams were prevalent as she held on for her life. The fur covered beast plunged a single finger into Mrs. Bradley's chest.

I continued to fire Corbin until the click of the falling

hammer was all that was left. The silver bullets didn't faze it. It swiftly cut through her chest with precision. Blood poured from the wound. The creature tossed away chunks of flesh and bone, immediately ripping out her heart. Mrs. Bradley went flaccid as it sank its teeth into the once strong, beating muscle. It howled toward the sky in satisfaction, tossing Mrs. Bradley some fifteen yards at our feet. The creature shot one last blood-filled grin at me as it scurried away into the darkness of the distant neighborhood.

"Aunt Nola, I haven't been that scared in a long time. I've never seen a werewolf like that before'" Jackson whispered. His eyes were wide and his breathing erratic. Jackson's hands quivered as he clutched the handle of Guardian.

The looks of shock on the other's faces told me they hadn't either. Charles and Jordan stood frozen; brows curled and mouths ajar. Tammy and Chloe were some distance behind us as tears fell from their eyes.

"I've seen one like that before. It looked a lot like—" My vision blurred as my eyes filled with tears. "It looked a lot like the werewolf that killed my parents and put this scar on my face."

CHAPTER
ELEVEN

"YOU GOT IT, CAPTAIN. IF WE SEE ANYTHING MORE, WE'LL GIVE YOU A CALL." — CHARLES

The revolving blue lights from the unmarked police cars reflected off the nearby homes in the neighborhood. A deluge of blood still poured from Mrs. Bradley's softball-sized chest wound covered the asphalt. Her lifeless eyes had turned a milky shade of white. The people of the neighborhood lingered outside and watched as Captain Martel and her squad questioned everyone. The neighbors all shared the same looks of shock and fear, as their minds were probably in the process of comprehending what they had seen. Raised and curled brows accompanied tear-filled eyes as everyone watched their neighbor laying cold and lifeless on the concrete. It wasn't all tearful. The Taylors glared at me in a manner so cold I could feel the tiny bumps along the outside of my arms. I had let them down. I let down Mrs. Bradley. The Taylor's thoughts were loud and clear.

If Nola couldn't protect a fragile old lady that lived next door to her, what use was she?

At least, that's what I surmised they were thinking. That

was what their facial expressions conveyed. Who knew? It could've been my own doubts infecting my perception of the situation.

The last thing I needed to deal with was the presumptions and arrogance of an overzealous cop. In each unpleasant encounter with Captain Martel, I noticed her wrinkled, stained clothes and questionable investigative techniques. Aligning us in the street, within the crime scene tape, a few feet from Mrs. Bradley's corpse, was unorthodox, to say the least. There was nothing to lie about. We all saw the lycanthrope. We all saw what it did to her. But to question us all together, well, that was just poor investigative technique. I wondered, how could anyone put this moron in charge of any specialized investigative unit? Knowing the type of cop her father was, he wouldn't be proud.

The other two officers that hovered over Mrs. Bradley popped open two cases that looked a lot like tackle boxes beside her. One officer pulled out a camera and took photos while the other collected and bagged the hairs left behind by the werewolf from Mrs. Bradley's wound. This was highly unusual without the presence of a crime lab on scene to do this type of processing. Nothing about what they were doing followed department procedures. It was as if they didn't have any protocols to follow. If that was the case, that would mean Captain Martel had carte blanche to handle things the way she saw fit. With that kind of unchecked power it made her even more problematic.

"Again, it looks like you and your little collection of cartoon characters' stories check out, Nola. Neighbors all gave the same story. My question is why couldn't you stop this thing? Aren't you the legendary hunter? Why am I looking at another dead body?" Captain Martel asked, still with an inappropriate smirk of satisfaction on her face. Her breath reeked of a combination of cigarettes and cough drops.

I suppressed the urge to put her in her place as I swallowed the excessive saliva that had built during the prolonged silence. It wasn't important now. "Better question. What are you and your squad going to do about this thing? These bodies have been piling up for some time now based on the information I received. Captain, you're the one who has the resources of the city behind you, and you have shit to show for it. Your only interest seems to be some sort of personal vendetta against me."

Martel's face softened a little as she noticed the stares from everyone in earshot. "We don't work for you. And I'm sure you've noticed the city has been slowly phasing out your services. City leadership knows what these attacks are, and we'll deal with it accordingly. You and your little investigative team can go back inside and stay out of our way. It's just a werewolf," Captain Martel said.

"It's not just a werewolf!" I yelled with a slight step toward her. "Stay out of your way? When have you ever seen a werewolf with the control to do something like that?" I pointed down at Mrs. Bradley's wound. "It's probably you pushing the brass to phase us out, but it's a mistake. You're out of your league. The damn thing was right next door to me and didn't make a sound, and—"

Charles placed his arm across my chest. Frozen, I stared at his large bicep with rage coursing through me. If I had the strength, I would have snapped it in two.

"You got it, Captain. If we see anything more, we'll give you a call," Charles said.

"Good." Captain Martel glared in my direction with a smug look of satisfaction. "At least one of you has some brains. You folks should get inside. The coroner is here, and we've just about wrapped up. It's not safe for any of you outside. You all might be better served to go and read some dusty old book or something? Isn't that what you do?"

The thump of the coroner's van doors as they slammed shut jolted me back to clarity. Captain Martel and her squad drove away, speeding unnecessarily down the neighborhood street as the once bright blue lights that illuminated the area faded in the distance.

"So, what? We all just come back inside and eat cake now? We should have gone after that thing," Jackson said, rapidly blinking his tearful eyes.

"And do what? Everyone in here saw what happened. It took those silver rounds as if it was nothing. We need a plan, and we need to figure out exactly what we're dealing with. Now is not the time to be hotheaded, Jackson." I placed my hands on his shoulders and forcefully sat him down in the chair nearby.

Jackson was fond of Mrs. Bradley, as she was of him. What he saw tonight appeared to cut deeper for him than the rest of us. Jackson needed to be monitored. I didn't need him going off half-cocked chasing that . . . thing throughout the city. Jackson was fearless, but his emotions sometimes made him reckless.

The faces around the room all shared a contorted look of either disbelief or terror. Well, except Charles. He appeared to be deep in thought and oblivious to what was going on around him. The room was still after Jackson's initial outburst.

The high-pitched ring of my cell phone assaulted the silence, along with the bright white glow of its screen displaying the familiar name across it. The Collector. The tone of the voice on the other end always exuded condescension and accompanied with cryptic messages.

"I take it you're the thing we saw tonight?" I asked after I answered the call.

There was no need for pleasantries. These harassing phone calls had been anything but pleasant.

"Sweet Nola, this is my last phone call. I've grown weary of playing this game. All of these years warning you, and you still failed when you had a chance to stop me. Everyone you know will suffer a painful death. Just like your parents. Just like your sister and just like your neighbor." The familiar deepened voice on the other end was doing its best to antagonize me.

"You're right about one thing. Our little conversations are over. I've entertained this long enough," I said, abruptly ending the call.

"Who was that?" Charles asked. He squinted as he glared at me.

Time to come clean with Charles and Jordan. I kept this from them all these years, and I was sure they wouldn't like it. Not one bit.

"Since the day we left Dalyville, I've been getting these strange and cryptic phone calls from the same phone number. I haven't been able to nail down a location or the person making the calls with a trace. The phone seems to be encrypted somehow. Almost like a VPN, the traces always bounce around with a different location every couple of minutes. I have no idea who it is on the other end. It's the usual rhetoric when he calls. 'I'm going to destroy your city. I'm going to kill everyone you love. You'll pay for killing so many of my children,'" I stammered at a rapid pace. "I'm talking real over-the-top, cheesy movie villain, type shit. Tonight, I suspected the lycanthrope responsible for Mrs. Bradley's death has been the one making all those calls. At least, in its human form."

Everyone's eyes lingered on me.

"What the hell do you mean? Has someone been threatening you? Threatening us all this time? And you kept it to yourself? Why would you do that?" Jordan asked, his face filled with disappointment after his barrage of questions. "That explains what happened the other night. I knew it wasn't a coincidence. I knew we were being targeted."

"Wait, what happened last night?" Charles asked.

Jordan's eyes darted in my direction.

I hung my head in disbelief. "After Jordan picked me up from jail and before I picked up Tammy from the airport, a werewolf attacked us. Jordan put it down. It's no big deal; neither of us were hurt. I didn't think it was appropriate to bring up with Jackson's birthday party so close," I said.

Tammy grabbed Chloe by the arm and gently pulled her to the sofa, leaning closer to her ear. "We better step out of the way and let them talk this through."

The noise of Jackson and Jordan as they discussed what I should or shouldn't have done faded into the background as I stared at Charles. He was still quiet. Not a word. After what I told them, Charles had nothing to say. That wasn't what I expected. Unfortunately, it had been going this way for the past few months. He was always a bit of an introverted person, but recently Charles had been distant and evasive.

"Nothing, Charles?" I asked. Jackson and Jordan's debate silenced.

"Secrets," Charles answered. He looked up from the floor. His eyes locked onto mine.

"What about them?"

"The secrets we're keeping from each other are going to get one of us killed."

"Going to get one of us killed? It just got one of us killed, asshole. Tell her!" Jackson yelled, stepping toward Charles.

"Tell me what?" I asked, my brow raised.

Charles quickly glanced in Jackson's direction. It was a look I had seen before, often from other cops when they wanted someone to shut up because they had said too much in front of the wrong person. The look often implied a future discussion at a later date, usually involving a police baton. I had never seen that look on Charles' face before, at least not pointed in Jackson's direction.

"I've been hunting … alone," Charles blurted out.

"What? Why" I asked, my face contorted in confusion.

"It's more than just hunting. He's hiding something," Jackson interrupted.

Charles' head snapped back in Jackson's direction, the tension in his jawline apparent. A breath of silence filled the air and passed.

"Kid, I'm sick of your attitude. First, you've been acting standoffish toward me, and now you've been following me. I get it. You lost your parents. Well, so did I. So did your aunt. But dead parents don't give you the right to be an asshole."

"Charles! What the hell is wrong with you?" Tammy yelled,

punching him on the shoulder. She jerked her hand back, wincing in pain. Tammy's attempt at reprimanding Charles seemed to cause her more harm than the target of her anger.

That was probably the first punch Tammy had ever thrown in her life. The sight amused me. I would have laughed if I weren't outraged by Charles' cruelty. The way he spoke to Jackson hurt and shocked me, but most of all, it pissed me off.

His recklessness with his words cut through Jackson. Watching him, I saw the tension in his face as he fought back tears. I would deal with that later. I needed to hear what else Charles had to say.

Charles widened his eyes as he glanced at the shocked faces around the room. His face softened at my reaction. "Kid, I apologize. I let my anger get the best of me." Charles walked into the far corner of the room, away from the others, away from me.

"If you really want to do this now, I will. It's obvious Jackson has poisoned your trust for me," Charles said.

"No, Charles. You poisoned the trust I had for you. Take accountability," I replied.

"A few months back, I was hunting . . . alone. Just trying to clear my head. Things weren't going well between us, Nola. You were pushing me away. I'm not sure if you realized what you were doing. Hunting and giving my all to my mother's legacy helped. I figured with or without you, I would turn her company into a billion-dollar corporation. Dalyville was a success, but it came at a great cost. I wanted out, Nola. So, I figured I'd focus on getting paid."

"This isn't a therapy session. Get to the point," Jackson interrupted.

"I'm getting there. Anyway, while out hunting, I came

across a body. Some poor homeless bastard had his heart cut out. I found him in one of those blighted apartment buildings in eastern New Orleans that's been abandoned since after the hurricane. It was the damnedest thing I'd ever seen. It didn't track with any creature I knew, so I figured whatever did it was human. Then I heard the wolf howl outside. At that point, I knew there was a big problem. There was no full moon, and I was alone. I got out of there as fast as I could."

I shook my head in disbelief. "That doesn't make any sense. Why'd you run and why didn't you tell me about this?"

"I just told you!" Charles snapped. "There was a howl of a werewolf, and there was no full moon. If it changed out of sync with the moon cycle and it did that type of precision kill, I knew it was different. I knew it could probably kill me."

"Why didn't you come to us with it? Why keep secrets?" I asked again.

"Why? Because of your parents, that's why. If I took care of this myself, it would save you from reliving those memories. I wanted to do it myself," Charles said.

"I don't need someone to psychoanalyze me. I need someone who doesn't lie to me. Charles, I'm getting the feeling there's still something you aren't telling me."

"I get it," Charles said, as his eyes shifted back and forth, doing what he could to avoid eye contact.

"Charles, what's going on?" Tammy asked. Her voice filled with concern.

"I thought this was about the money. I thought together we could revitalize this city and make hundreds of millions of dollars in the process. I could retire. Leave the company in Tammy's hands, and move you and Jackson away to someplace nice. Somewhere we could be a family." Charles fell into the chair behind him. His shoulders slumped as his eyes fixated on me.

"All the werewolves we've encountered so far have changed outside of the full moon. Something different is involved here," I added, avoiding Charles' fixation on money.

"I later realized it wasn't a coincidence. This all started around the same time he came to town. The way he took an interest in my family. It seemed off," Charles said.

With a clenched fist and tense jaw, the warm sensation of the blood rushing to my face consumed me as my heart pounded feverishly.

"Who, Charles?" Tammy yelled.

"Frank."

CHAPTER
TWELVE

"IS THAT WHAT THIS PATHETIC ATTEMPT TO INTIMIDATE ME IS ALL ABOUT?"—FRANK

Thursday—Five days before Mardi Gras

The recollection of what happened last night had Charles pacing his office in anticipation of his colleague's visit, tapping his left pant pocket with his hand as he paced back and forth. This could all blow up in his face, and all the work Charles put into building upon his mother's legacy and the fortune could fall apart. There was a chance Frank's presence was just a coincidence. Unlikely. That wasn't what Charles' gut was telling him. There were too many coincidences. Besides, Nola had enough heartache, and he needed to make up for some of his misguided decisions he made recently.

"She really needs to trust me more. I can take care of this myself. I can't allow more pain to happen to her. Nola's PTSD is serious enough. I'm not sure how much more she can handle. Especially since—"

The buzz of the phone intercom interrupted his thoughts.

"Mr. Jones, Mr. Lopez is here to see you," the soft voice on the other end of the intercom said.

"Okay. Send him in."

Charles buttoned his charcoal-colored suit coat and tucked his ocean blue necktie inside as he scurried behind his desk and sat. Everything in his office was in perfect position. Organized. Clean. An environment where he had control, and all the power behind it was his to yield.

Let's see if you are who you say you are.

"Charles, my good man, how are you doing today?" Frank asked, his hand extended. His smile seemed carefree.

Charles raised his brow at the unexpected pleasantries. The fact that Frank would start this meeting with everyday greetings and not move directly into the sights of what happened at the cafe caught Charles off guard, suspicious even. He decided to indulge Frank.

"I'm good. Ready to solidify some of the plans we have in motion and revitalize this city . . . and make a ton of cash. There's no better time to start breaking ground on new plans than the carnival season," Charles replied, standing and extending his arm to shake Frank's hand. "Have you made your way down to Bourbon Street or caught a parade yet?"

"Not yet. I prefer to watch from afar. It's not my idea of a good time. I would indulge only if out of necessity."

"I understand. Also, my associate, Tammy Hodges, is in town. I know you two have spoken before, mostly through correspondence, but I think it would be great if you two met in person finally. She does most of the business out of the New York office and covers the land overview in Dalyville. Her input on any of our projects would be invaluable. She's the only person whose opinion I would put above my own, outside of my mother's, of course."

Frank's well-maintained teeth appeared briefly at Charles' statement. A type of forced grin that was done out of professional pleasantry rather than a natural occurrence. Frank sat on the chair on the other side of the desk, unyielding in his eye contact. Frank leaned back slightly into his chair and glanced at the picture of Charles' mother that sat in a frame on his desk.

"Yes, she was a remarkable woman. Tenacious and a force to be reckoned with when it came to business. She had quite a reputation. The loss of a parent is a pain never forgotten. Luckily, based on what you've told me and from what I've seen with my own eyes from Nola, your family cup should now be overflowing with love?" Frank asked.

"Yes, I'm grateful to have them in my life. They keep me grounded and on the proper path," Charles replied.

"I'm sure what happened last night must have scared them pretty good. It was horrific and unfortunate what happened to your neighbor, but luckily, you, Nola, and Jackson came away alright. At least, that's what the news reported," Frank said.

Charles interlocked his fingers and leaned forward on his desk. "News report. What news report are you referring to? What happened last night didn't make the news. How do you know about it, Frank?"

Frank presented a crooked smile. "I'm not quite sure what you mean? I heard it from your local radio news broadcast. The report said its sources were eyewitnesses. I'm sure with an identified dead body in the morgue, it made it easy for a reporter to verify. Based on the smug look on your face, you were expecting to catch me in a lie. That's not nice, Charles."

Charles' gaze lingered on Frank, unmoved by his explanation. "Frank, before we get down to business, why is it you ask about my family whenever we meet? What's with the obsession?" Absent a smile, Charles glared at Frank. It lingered. His stare could pierce its target purely for the purpose of intimidation.

Frank's bright smile and perfect teeth followed, only visible for a few moments. Frank's eyes locked on Charles again. The glare was something Charles used often when dealing with other soldiers within his own ranks back in the army. Soldiers often tested each other to see how much they could get away with. The stare downs didn't last long and often led to an immediate understanding, or sometimes it was taken to the next physical level. No one wanted to be seen as the one who backed down.

Frank didn't seem interested in backing down. He glared back at Charles, his face void of emotion. No anger. No obvious tell of determination to outdo Charles at his own game. He just stared back... with a coldness.

"I always ask because it's what you talk about most often. Your family, hunting, and always last, your business. It seems to me the easiest way to relate to you is to talk about your family. I understand that. I understand people. I have a family of my own," Frank replied.

"Do you? You never mentioned them. In all this time we've worked together, you've never mentioned them."

"You never asked. Honestly, you're a pretty self-absorbed, and slightly arrogant individual. What do you want to know? I don't have a wife, but I have two kids, a son and a daughter. I'm willing to do anything to make sure they have everything they need and are protected. Protected, even from themselves, if necessary. Just like any father worth his salt," Frank answered.

"So will I. Let me speak plainly. I hope you can understand this, since you are aware of what I do outside of this business. Also, given what happened that day at the cafe and what happened last night with my neighbor, you can understand what we're up against. These werewolf attacks... If I recall correctly, it all started when you came to New Orleans. I knew about them early on, even before Nola. From what I can tell, these lycanthropes seem to be taunting us. Toying with us by either attacking us directly or attacking those around us. You wouldn't know anything about that, would you?" Charles' stare again lingered on Frank.

Frank slid down in the chair as he let out an obnoxious laugh that filled the room and leaked out into the reception area in earshot of Charles' executive assistant. With the bottom portion of his index finger, Frank wiped away the water that fell from his eyes as he continued to laugh almost uncontrollably.

"Is that what this pathetic attempt to intimidate me is all about? You think I know something about the werewolves in this city? What, you think I'm one of them? Bad news Chucky boy. I'm well put together on the outside, but I can barely walk long distances without my hip giving out. Sorry, I'm not your guy." Frank stood and walked toward the door. "I was there when that thing attacked the cafe. If you recall, I was scared shitless, just like most of the people there. I had more respect for what you did as a hunter after seeing that thing up close, but now you look pathetic. Not sure if I want to move forward with our projects if you lack this much attention to detail and insight. You are definitely not your mother. I'll be in touch."

Frank slammed the door as he left. Charles clenched his jaw and shook his head after a few moments of reflecting on how badly that went for him and the firm. Still, his instincts were telling him Frank knew something. It appeared to be more than a coincidence that he was here.

Frank looked scared that day at the cafe. If he saw the werewolf last night, he probably would have soiled himself.

Charles had seen a lycanthrope like that before.

"Maybe I should let Nola know some of the things I'm aware of, and we can nail this thing together," Charles mumbled.

The city's supernatural task force was useless. Always there after the fact. The phone on his desk rang.

"Damnit, it's like Nola is watching me," Charles mumbled before he grabbed the receiver and answered.

"How'd it go?" the voice on the other end asked.

"Nola, Frank knows something. He mentioned last night and how happy he was that the family was okay. There was no media out there, and detective numb-nuts cleaned up the scene before anyone could get out there. He tried to give some weak excuse when I pushed him on it. I wasn't buying it. So, how did he know about last night?"

CHAPTER
THIRTEEN

"MILLER, YOU BETTER BE SURE IF YOU PULL THE TRIGGER."—CAPTAIN MARTEL

"We're losing light. Get your asses moving. The anonymous tip said it saw something massive that moved like an animal that crawl into the back of the building. Reminder, if this is what we think it is, this son-of-a-bitch killed a citizen last night," Martel barked her orders after she and her team stepped out of their squad cars. "We're gonna do what that bitch Nola Maor couldn't do for her own next-door neighbor. Kill this thing and protect our citizens. We will not mimic her incompetence. This ends tonight. The building has three entrances, so, two-man teams. You two in the rear. You two catch the roof access from the fire escape, and Miller, you'll come with me. We'll take the front entrance."

Captain Martel's dictatorial voice echoed off the exterior walls of the abandoned building as she barked orders and directed her team into position. The clumsy sounds of the boots from her poorly trained team sounded like a marching band stomping its way down a parade route. Once a thriving store, the abandoned building sat near the busy interstate that ran through eastern New Orleans, separated only by a small service road and parking lot. The former two-story kitchen and bathroom supply store was once a staple of Saturday afternoon homeowners and elderly couples that loved to window-shop and browse the latest fixtures and tile designs. The emerald-colored stucco exterior was littered with graffiti and an occasional broken window.

"Goddamnit. It would have been nice if this tip would have come a little earlier in the day. We've lost all the daylight, and it's probably darker than the depths of hell inside there," Captain Martel said.

Officer Miller stood next to her and laughed at Martel's statement. The laugh was dry and timid. She knew she had a reputation to be childish and vengeful. Rumors traveled throughout the police department about her notorious ability to hold a grudge. The rumors were true. Martel knew Miller forced his laugh to stay in her good graces but she also knew Miller didn't like her very much. She often catch him rolling his eyes when she entered the room he happened to be in. Martel didn't mince her words when she spoke to subordinates and knew she wasn't well liked because of it. Martel once overheard Miller refere to her as a walking cliche. One of those officers drunk off the power of the badge rather than one interested in doing the job of service and protection to the people of New Orleans. Since that day she decided to keep Miller close and when the timing was right, make his life a living hell.

"Ma'am, do you want left or right flank?"

"You take the left, Officer Miller, and keep your flashlight out of my face," Martel ordered.

The building's double glass front door entrance had Captain Martel and Officer Miller posted on each side. Miller pulled his service firearm and flashlight from their respective holsters and placed his back against the wall. Captain Martel posted against the right side of the door with her radio and handgun in hand.

"Everyone in position?" she whispered, keying her radio. The hum of cars traveling at high speeds along Interstate 10 consumed the brief stillness of the night's air.

"Ready to go, Captain."

"Go, now!"

Officer Miller took point through the double glass door with Martel close behind him. Inside was much more subdued, much gloomier, damp, and putrid. The dank odor of mold from years of infiltration by rainwater stained the tiled ceiling and drywall. As Captain Martel and Officer Miller scanned their flashlights around the room, an assorted array of food wrappers and graffiti covered the floor. The sight of it told the story of the different squatters that took shelter inside. Dozens of rats scurried along the floor near their feet. Captain Martel danced in place to avoid the fur covered scavengers, biting her lips to suppress her scream. Martel took a deep breath and exhaled slowly once the rats cleared.

She placed two fingers at eye level and waved them forward at Officer Miller, ordering him to continue deeper inside. Their visibility was now restricted to the mercy of the areas their flashlights could cover.

"Miller, you better be sure if you have to pull the trigger. Our team is in here. We don't need any accidents because you're scared," Captain Martel whispered. Her comments were provoked by the timid steps Miller took in front of her.

"Oh, god. What's that smell?" Miller whispered. He covered his nose with the back of the hand holding his service weapon.

Captain Martel closed her eyes and turned her head to maneuver away from the odor. The stench of death intensified the deeper inside they ventured. Miller gagged and his body convulsed before he eventually gave in, vomiting where he stood. Eyes watering, Captain Martel exhaled deeply as she moved her flashlight back and forth in front of her, passing Miller and illuminating the base of a stairwell, past the old, empty display shelves beside her.

"There's no mistaking that smell. That's decomp, and it's close," Martel said.

The unexpected high-pitched screams of two men in the distance above jarred Captain Martel and Officer Miller. Both panned their flashlights to the right, deeper into the darkness of the building.

"Who was that?" Miller stammered. His hands trembled. "Hunt! Rhodes! Haynes! Bro . . . "

"Miller, shut the hell up," Martel interrupted, her voice well above a whisper. "That thing's in here. You're giving away our position."

Another set of screams sounded out from above their heads, followed by deafening silence. Both panned their flashlights at the base of the staircase. Miller inched his flashlight up the stairs one at a time until it reached the top. Blood poured down the stairs like a crimson slinky, thinning at the drop on every stair below. The lights trembled in sync with their hands.

"Let's get the hell out of here and get some back-up. We can make sure it doesn't get out of the building, and we can nail this thing with S.W.A.T. on the scene," Miller argued, his voice shaky and eyes wide.

"Absolutely not. You're equipped with enough silver bullets

to afford a small mansion. We're gonna go up those stairs, help the rest of the squad, and put about forty or fifty bullets in its hairy ass. It's nothing but a damn big dog. Get your shit together and make good use of all that melted down and repurposed jewelry."

"Dogs don't slice people open like a sharp knife through a melon with its claws, Martel."

Captain Martel grabbed Miller by the collar and shoved him ahead of her up the stairs. The rancid stench of decomposition strengthened and caused a stinging and burning sensation inside of her nose. Officer Miller and Captain Martel slowly ascended to the top of the stairs. Somehow, the area was darker than the space downstairs. Martel's eyes watered at the stench. Officer Miller widened his eyes at the sight of carnage illuminated by the shine of his flashlight. The stack of mutilated bodies across the room on the far wall were in different stages of rotting.

"Oh my gawd! T-there must be t-twenty or thirty bodies up here," Miller stuttered. Sweat dripped down the side of his face.

Martel tapped him on his shoulder and flashed a light in his face. Her index finger pressed against her lips as she moved the flashlight over to the other side of the room. Officer Miller and Captain Martel's uniformed co-workers laid piled on top of each other with the other intermingled limbs of rotted corpses. Blood poured from their wounds and pooled near the center of the room. Their shredded bodies paled at the loss.

"My God. Hunt. Rhodes. That has to be Haynes and Broadway. Their faces look like they were mauled by some animal." Miller turned toward her. "Fuck you."

"What?" Captain Martel asked. Her brow curled.

"You heard me loud and clear. *Fuck you*. Time for me to go.

I'm not dying for this. I'm not dying following you." Miller turned and quickly descended the staircase. His rapid footsteps became faint as he ran outside.

Martel's hand gripped the handle of her gun a little tighter. The sound of her labored breaths monopolized her ears. Fear weaved its way throughout her body. The sporadic, panicked sounds of her breaths that echoed in her ears were short-lived. The low, subtle growl that emanated from the blackness on the other side of the room. Hands shaking, Martel panned her flashlight from side to side. Her breaths were more erratic. Martel's heart pounded violently in her chest.

Emerging from the darkness was the glow of a set of fire-burning red eyes and sharp, blood-covered canine teeth. The thump of the figure's massive paws as it smacked against the tile floor, out of the darkness and into the brightness of Captain Martel's flashlight, caused her to jolt with every step.

"That's no dog," she mumbled, dropping her gun to the floor.

A growl emitted from the beast. The sound reverberated in her chest. The heat and stench of its breath smacked against her face. The smell mimicked the odor of rotten eggs and caused her to become nauseate.

"You don't belong here," it said, with a deep voice, blended with a growl.

"P-please. P-please don't," Captain Martel pleaded, as tears fell from her eyes.

"I like when they beg. You walked into the wrong den."

Martel dropped to the tile floor, into the pool of blood, as she reached for her gun. The still warm thickened fluid clung to her tactical clothing as she struggled to gather her footing.

The beast kicked her in the stomach, forcing her to slide

across the room. Her body slammed against the mound of bodies a dozen feet away. Martel screamed in anguish as she clutched at her gut. The intense pain felt as if her organs had exploded from the force. Pieces of flesh from the bodies above fell on top of her. A maggot-infested piece of rotting flesh from a body toppled into Martel's mouth. She struggled to breathe and spat at its rancid taste.

The claws of the creature ripped into Martel's gut and lifted her from under the bodies. Blood spewed from her mouth as she coughed.

"I thought you came here to play. You're no hunter. Just a waste of my time. Just an intruder. Usually, I would indulge on your heart. You see, it's the premium cut of the human body. Not you. You smell . . . sour," the beast said as it bared its teeth.

The creature dropped Martel to the floor. Her innards spilled on impact. As she clutched at her stomach, Martel managed to stand while the werewolf towered in front of her. The blackened nails of its predatory hand reached toward the ceiling; her body frozen. Red fluid sprayed across the monster's face after the claws came down upon her and sliced open her neck. She grabbed at her throat, gasping for air. Martel gargled as the open cavity filled with blood. The fluid that choked her drowned out her screams for help.

She fell to the floor. The slowing rhythmic sound of her heartbeat felt comforting. Then, silence.

CHAPTER
FOURTEEN

"I'M NOT SURE. I HAVEN'T OPENED IT. I'M AFRAID OF WHAT IT WILL SAY."—CHARLES

F riday—Four days before Mardi Gras

The early morning frenzy of people colonizing city property with the use of ladders, tables, and even the yellow caution tape used for construction and crime scenes was used to claim the best parts of sidewalk and median space. In preparation for the weekend parades, citizens hunted for the best viewing position. The closer the position to the front of the crowd, nearest to the parade floats, the better a person's chances were of catching the most idolized throws in the parade. The weekend before Fat Tuesday was no doubt the most rambunctious couple of days for the city of New Orleans, outside of Jazz Fest.

All it meant for Charles was an unnecessary noise that disturbed an already unrestful sleep. Truth be told, Charles hadn't slept well since the events in Tennessee and his encounter with Nola. Nights plagued with vicious nightmares and sweat as his body tossed and turned from one side of the bed to the other were anything but a peaceful rest.

Charles leaned against the wall of the kitchen; his eyelids were heavy as he stared at the coffeepot. The sizzle of the automatic coffee maker as it squeezed out the last few drops of java juice into the cup put a slight crooked smile on Charles' face. No cream. No sugar. Black and dark roasted. He hoped it cleared the morning fog from his brain.

Charles was well aware of the severe mistakes he had committed in life. He had made far too many. Some he regretted. Others, not so much. Thoughts of the people he had hurt in the past flooded his head. He closed his eyes tightly and pushed down on his temple with the base of his hand.

The army had allowed him to execute government retribution under the disguise of orders. He enjoyed it. He was good at it, with a special thank you for all his natural talents. Charles had trouble coping with the punishments he dished out outside of the cover of his military duty. Those were the things he had been fighting, things he regretted the most. Especially the one self-initiated mission he completed. There was once a time when Charles delighted in the memory of the blood bath from that day. The sound of the screams and the agony on the faces of the targets as they bled haunted him. He buried those memories away in the far corner of his soul and did his best to keep that pain from Nola, for both their sakes.

Steam rose from his cup. Charles took two large gulps of coffee. The searing pain, scalded tongue and burned roof of his mouth, served as a small, just punishment for his past actions, and he welcomed it.

Dalyville was a high price to pay for clarity. That place took his mother, then that thing took his mother's face and used it to kill most of Nola's remaining family. It took a father and a mother away from Jackson. A relatable pain for Charles. It took a sister and a brother away from the woman he loved and compounded the trauma she carried from her past. The scar on her face was a constant reminder of the day her parents were taken from her. Charles' made it his personal mission since then had been to fix as much as he could. First, to be someone Nola could depend on, and love. Second, to be a father figure for Jackson and a friend. He knew the struggles of growing up without a father. It wasn't a fate that Jackson deserved. Lastly, he wanted to earn as much money as possible and make sure they didn't have to worry about finances ever again. His success in his intention was spotty at best in his eyes. Still too many lies, too much trauma, and too many secrets between the three of them to make the family Charles wanted.

His shoulders slumped as he took another swallow of coffee. The burn was satisfying.

"Good morning! I see everyone has gotten an early start today," Tammy said. Her blonde hair was the textbook picture of bed head, with its ends reaching out in every direction. Her pink cotton pajamas struggled to cling to her tiny frame.

"Good morning, Tammy. I see you still refuse to buy pajamas that fit?" Charles asked with a sly smile.

"Don't be a jerk so early in the morning. You know I love the blanket feeling of oversized PJs. What's going on with you? I know when that vein in your forehead makes an appearance, there's a problem."

Tammy poured her own cup of coffee into a mug that featured a cartoon vampire and the phrase 'I swear it's just coffee' printed under it. She poured a significant amount of creamer inside the mug, followed by four, maybe five scoops of sugar.

The mug definitely belongs to Jackson.

"Do you want some coffee with that cake mix?" Charles smirked.

"What? Don't be a douchebag." Tammy laughed.

"There's the real Tammy. People still buying that sweet girl act?" Charles asked.

"Whatever gets me ahead. When the men of the business world don't see you as a threat, they let their guard down. That's when I grab them by the balls and squeeze . . . tight."

Charles snorted with laughter. "Yeah, that's the Tammy I know."

"Where is everyone?"

"Nola and Jackson left with Jordan to research Frank and the Lycanthrope more extensively. I don't expect them to be back for a while."

"Why didn't you tag along? You're the one who's spent the most time with him. I'm sure there's some insight on Frank you could have given. Jackson told me you haven't been part of the team lately," Tammy said.

"I doubt he put it that nicely," Charles replied.

"He didn't. But you should expect that. Jackson is a man now. Nola is all the family he has left, and hunting is what gives him purpose. If you've been spotty at being there for them lately, he's going to react. He's going to protect his auntie and himself. Is that what's bothering you?" Tammy sat next to Charles at the kitchen table.

Charles nervously tapped the front right-side pocket of his jeans. "I miss Mama," he replied, his leg shaking.

"We both do. She was a remarkable woman."

"She left me a letter. I found it when I went through her things back in New York."

Charles pulled the letter from his pant pocket and showed it to Tammy. The white envelope was folded, wrinkled, and had bent corners.

"A letter? What does it say?" Tammy asked, grabbing for Charles' hand.

"I'm not sure. I haven't opened it. Kind of afraid of what it will say."

"Why? She obviously wanted you to have it. It has your name on it, right?" Tammy asked.

"A little more than that." Charles unfolded the envelope to reveal his mother's handwriting on the front. He let Tammy read the front of the envelope.

To Charles: Read only upon my untimely death. You deserve to know.

"Charles Dalyville happened four years ago. You've been holding on to this envelope all this time?"

"Tammy, you know about some of the things I've done. You've been the sister I needed since my mother hired you. I've been dealing with so much. I just don't know if I have room for anything else. Now my attempt to solidify my family's legacy could have brought this asshole into our lives."

"You mean Frank?" Tammy asked, placing a comforting hand on his shoulder.

"Yes!" Charles yelled in reply. "It can't be a coincidence that he showed up, and these things came back to New Orleans. Frank's got something to do with this. If he isn't behind this, then they're targeting him as well. Either way, getting into business with him was a mistake."

"You vetted him, right? You used the usual company

resources to vet him. Everything about him checked out. His wealth, business, and identity. Everything about him checked out, right, Charles?" Tammy asked. A slight tone of frustration sounded in her voice.

"There is no vetting process within the business to check for lycanthropy," Charles replied.

"So, you're saying you think he is—"

Charles nodded with a raised brow.

"Well, the crew is on it now. If there's anything to find, they will find it. You can't hide anything from Nola. She eventually finds out about everything." Tammy stood from the table and finished the last of her coffee.

"Not everything," Charles replied, his cell phone now vibrating against the table. The screen illuminated the name Frank Lopez across it.

"Speak of the devil." Charles picked up the phone with a sigh. "Hello, Frank. I didn't think we had a meeting..."

"Charles, I was attacked last night," Frank interrupted.

Charles quickly stood from the table. His brow tightened as his eyes shifted back and forth from Tammy.

"Are you okay?" Charles asked while he listened.

"I'm okay. It was a werewolf, and it managed to slice open my leg," Frank replied.

"I'm on my way," Charles said, ending the call.

"What's going on?" Tammy asked.

"It seems a werewolf attacked Frank last night. Get dressed. Since this involves the business as well, I want you with me."

Charles knocked on the door of room 101A, one of two penthouse suites that shared an entire floor of the luxury hotel located in downtown New Orleans. Tammy stood beside him and looked around at the significantly improved décor from any hotel she had the pleasure of staying in, luxury or not. The ocean blue carpet was thick and plush. It almost gave the impression that her feet were walking on clouds. The door and its surroundings copied the entrance to a French designed New Orleans mansion with a well-done doorknocker attached.

"Who's there?" the voice on the other side of the door yelled.

"It's Charles."

The door opened, and there stood Frank with a single crutch supporting his left side. His tall frame was slightly bent to reach the crutch handle. Frank's shorts fell halfway down his thigh and revealed a partially blood-soaked bandage wrapped around his leg. His mood reflected that of a man that wasn't used to being hobbled in any way, as he turned his back toward Charles and Tammy and made his way back to the sofa. The volume on the television was unusually loud. Some raunchy reality TV show was playing. A man of Frank's education and culture didn't seem to be the type to indulge in that type of programming. He lowered the volume a bit as he sat, grabbing the halfway filled glass with an amber liquid.

"Glad you could make it, Charles. Who's the young lady with you?" Frank asked. His face was void of expression.

"This is Tammy Hodges. You had a couple of correspondence with her before. She runs the New York branch," Charles answered.

"That's right. I remember you now. I always wondered why

Charles waded in the muddy waters here in New Orleans, while you ran the big show in New York," Frank said, his brow slightly raised.

"Watch yourself. Ms. Hodges is very capable, and she's like a sister to me. Don't overstep," Charles replied.

The corners of Frank's mouth moved slightly as he glared at Tammy. Her shoulders shifted as her eyes cut away.

"Ms. Hodges, my apologies. I'm in pain. It's a reminder of what I've been dragged into. I assume you know of Charles' extracurricular activities?"

"If you mean his hunting, then yes, I'm aware." Tammy answered.

Charles walked around the coffee table and sat in the chair nearest Frank. He glanced at him, trying to get a better look at his leg. "Frank, what happened?"

"One of those things attacked me. I was walking back to the hotel after dinner, and it came out of a piss-filled alleyway. It was just as nasty as that werewolf from the cafe. It scratched at me. I got out of the way just in time, scratching my leg on the jagged metal edge of the dumpster I ran into. If it wasn't for a large crowd of paradegoers that walked by and scared it off, I'd be dead right now. All because you brought your craziness into my life," Frank said.

"That doesn't make any sense. A bloodthirsty werewolf had you in its sights, and a crowd of passersby scared it off?" Tammy asked.

"I don't give a damn what you think. I have the deep laceration to prove it." Frank replied, grabbing at his leg. He grimaced. "I don't remember asking you here, anyway. Charles, I think our partnership is done for the time being. Take your little make-believe sister and leave. Do me a favor. If you ever decide to leave this hunting foolishness behind, give me a call and we can make some real money together."

Charles shook his head and watched as Frank took another sip from the glass. "I thought you were interested in what I do on the side. Two up close and personal encounters with a werewolf, and that's it? Tail between your legs, running at the first sign of a little adversity. How'd you manage to gain as much as you have in life?" Charles asked.

"By being smart. Something it seems you're lacking," Frank answered.

The sound emanating from the television changed from the stagnant voices of commercials peddling their products to the repetitive melody of the noon news broadcast introduction. Frank stared at the screen, his face void of emotion.

"Good afternoon, New Orleans. We have breaking news of a gruesome and tragic scene in eastern New Orleans. Five members of a special city task force have been found brutally murdered in an abandoned building. One member of the task force is currently missing and wanted for questioning. In addition, from the information we're gathering from officials on the scene, at least another twelve bodies were found stacked on each other inside. All of the bodies are in various stages of decomposition. Our field reporter..."

Frank extended the remote and powered off the television, taking another large sip from his glass. The television was now silent like the rest of the room.

"It looks like you and your woman's lack of effectiveness as hunters cost more people their lives. A shame. I need you and your pretend sister to leave." Frank stood and limped to the door, holding it open.

"I'll be in touch, Frank. Before I go, do you want me to take a look at your wound? I can clean it up a bit and put some fresh bandages on it," Charles said.

"Are you a doctor?" Frank asked, a brow raised and a smirk on his face.

"Of course not, but I have some training."

"Right." Frank shook his head as he hobbled his way back to his chair. "Goodbye, Chuck."

"Yeah, I didn't think so." Charles reached into his pocket for his phone. He and Tammy left the hotel room.

The thump of the slamming door jolted Tammy's shoulders. Charles held the phone to his ear as it rang on the other end.

"Hello," the voice on the other end answered.

"Nola, turn on the news. Something took out Captain Martel and the task force."

CHAPTER
FIFTEEN
"THAT WOULD EXPLAIN THE TWO DIFFERENT STYLES OF MURDERS." — JORDAN

I raced back across the hall and opened the door to the study. The cool air from the air conditioning rushed against my face as I entered. A bit of a relief from the warmth of the blood flowing feverishly through me as my heart raced at the news.

"Guys, that was Charles. He's telling me the news just reported that five of the six members of the task force are dead. One is missing, and they found at least another twelve bodies or so in some abandoned building in eastern New Orleans."

"Twelve bodies? They've been here longer than we thought," Jordan said, his brow raised.

"He didn't say, but I'd have to guess that when they start to identify the bodies, there's a good chance a few of them will be missing persons cases," I replied.

Jackson closed the book laid it out in front of him. He stood at the news. "What type of werewolf takes out an entire police task force armed with silver bullets? Did the report give any more details?"

"Frank cut off the information before Charles could learn more. He was visiting Frank at the time of the news broadcast."

"What?" Jackson and Jordan yelled in sync.

"Calm down. I knew about the visit. Charles called me before he met with him. He and Tammy went there because he claimed to be attacked by a werewolf. The news alert happened while he was there," I said.

I walked over, sat behind my desk, and opened the laptop. Focused, my fingers feverishly pounded away at the keyboard to find more information about the murders. There had to be more out there. All headlines and articles from the past few months were vague and lacked details.

"It looks like the city has it on lock. It's Mardi Gras' biggest weekend, but I don't know what they'll do. I don't expect them to kick tourists out and shut the city down." I stood and closed the laptop, rubbing my hands together and exhaling sharply. "Charles didn't seem too convinced with Frank's story, so we need to ramp this up and find out more about the lycanthrope that killed Mrs. Bradley. Then we need to find out as much about Frank as we can. We don't know if the cases are connected or not, but let's go on the assumption that they are."

I pulled the sterling silver crucifix from under my blouse and rubbed it between my thumb and middle finger. "What do we know? There have been at least three werewolf attacks in the past week. The threatening phone calls over the last few years have all but stopped, except for the night Mrs. Bradley was killed. There has to be a pack in town. We don't know how many are in the pack, but the Alpha is definitely different," I said.

Jackson eagerly interjected, "Well, at least two of those

smelly curs have been put down, so there are two less than what they started with."

"That would explain the two different styles of murders. The more savage dismemberments and those with the hearts ripped out. We saw with our own eyes what's responsible for those," Jordan added.

Jackson scribbled in a notepad in front of him. His eyes softened, and a slight grin was apparent. I could practically see the wheels as they turned in his head. The sight was familiar. It was Janice all over again.

"Old," Jackson mumbled.

"What?" Jordan asked.

"Old. I think we are dealing with something old. Or something new, but my money is on something old." Jackson tapped the tip of his pen on his notepad.

"Jackson, I think you may be on to something. We've pretty much eradicated lycanthropes from this city. There was never an issue with silver not being effective. There's something more to these events than this thing being an Alpha werewolf in a pack. It has more strength, and it seems more aware in its wolf form than any normal werewolf. Not to mention it can change outside of the moon cycle, and it goddamn spoke," I said.

Jordan walked a little closer to me and stood on the other side of the desk. "The other werewolves changed outside of the full moon as well. The silver was effective on those creatures. Some changed during daylight, even. How can we explain that? What do we know about these things? A bite passes its infection. Silver in any form usually puts them down permanently—"

"Decapitation works damn well. No silver needed," Jackson interrupted, a sly grin on his face.

"Whatever the gray werewolf is, maybe it shares its power or something. Maybe the lesser werewolves can draw power from the larger one, and it allows them to change at will. There is something else that could be effective. Wolfsbane. It weakens them as well. Although I've never had the chance to use any. It's also pretty hard to come by." I opened the bottom drawer on the right side of the desk and pulled out the cheap, brown cardboard cigar box inside. As I removed the top, inside were several dried out lavender colored flowers inside. "Aconitum Variegatum, also known as Wolfsbane."

"Nola Maor." Jordan smiled after saying my name. "The woman is always prepared," he said. Jordan stared in my direction. He looked at me with adoration in his eyes.

"It's not the wolf that will give us answers. It's the wolf disguised as a certain man or woman that has all the answers we need," I said.

"You think Mama's journal might have some answers?" Jackson asked.

"Yes." I flipped through the pages. "We had a few conversations about some of the big three predators out there. Vampires, werewolves, and zombies."

"Zombies aren't real!" Jordan laughed.

"No. They aren't real. But we used the zombie lore to think about the other two in a different way. For instance, zombie lore usually involves a virus and always has a patient zero. Their infection is passed with a bite or scratch. Well, both werewolves and vampires make more of their own kind through a bite, just like zombies. Vampires are a little more involved, making their victims drink their blood as well," I said.

"Okay, I get it. But what does the transmission of a virus have to do with anything?" Jordan asked.

"My point has more to do with patient zero. Who was the first werewolf? How did it come to be? How many types are there? Given the lack of effectiveness of silver, I think these are the questions we need to ask. My sister— your mother—asked those questions, Jackson."

Jackson stood and turned toward the corner of the room with his back toward us. His hands reached for his eyes time and again.

"Sweetheart, are you okay?" I stood and made my way toward him.

"I'm good. Just dusty in here with all these old books." Jackson turned and sat back down at the makeshift table by his notepad, eyes slightly red. "Did you and Mom figure out anything?"

"Janice traced possible lycanthrope incidents back thousands of years. All the way back to Italy." I held the journal up to the brief two-page entry and showed it to Jordan and Jackson. "I remember the point she made that really hit home with me, which made me look at werewolves in a different way. Most of what we deal with has passed through death's door. Once alive and now a part of the undead in some form or fashion, except for two things: werewolves and demons. Demons were born in the underworld, werewolves walk the line between the living and the underworld," I said.

"I never really thought about it that way. So, what's the point?" Jordan interjected.

The cool air of the room helped calm me as I inhaled deeply from frustration. This group had worked together long enough that I shouldn't have to spoon-feed the information to them.

Jordan's brow lifted at what I could only guess was the sight of my irritation with them.

"Auntie, with all due respect, we've only been at this for about four years, but I know you're frustrated, so we depend on you to get us through this," Jackson said. He turned as he glared at me.

Both Jackson's and Jordan's eyes were affixed in my direction.

"Guys, forgive me. This thing has been taunting me since Dalyville, and now it's living up to its threats. I'm just tired." I lowered my head briefly. "The point I was trying to make was that if Jackson and Janice are right, and we're looking at something old and once human, its power could be commensurate with its age. It's possible this thing is hundreds, if not thousands, of years old."

"That's impossible. Werewolves aren't immortal," Jordan paused with a look of concern. "Are they?" he asked.

"We don't really know. We don't really know a lot about the origins of the lycanthrope. But if there is another species of werewolf out there, it was only a matter of time before we ran into one. I think this is what we're dealing with."

"And somehow, over four years ago, you pissed it off to the point that it wanted to stalk you and hunt you?" Jordan asked.

"The last werewolf I encountered was the one that killed my parents and put this scar on my face. It was stronger than I had ever seen, and silver didn't affect it either. It didn't look like the one we saw. The color of the fur was different. It almost killed me. Why is it coming after us now? I don't know."

The room fell silent as Jackson and Jordan stared at one another. Both of them coughed softly, as if they struggled to find the words to provide comfort or a solution. Jackson opened his mouth with a slight pause.

"What did Charles say about Frank, again? He was being sketchy and was conveniently present when the attacks started," Jackson asked.

"Charles and Tammy told me that someone attacked him last night. He was injured, but not bitten, and he survived. He's pretty pissed about it all. I'm not sure I buy it," I answered.

"Well, what do we do now?" Jordan asked.

"Jordan, I really don't know. For the first time in a long time, I don't have a plan, and that scares me."

CHAPTER
SIXTEEN
"MAYBE THIS WASN'T SUCH A GOOD IDEA?" —
NOLA

Sunday—Two days before Mardi Gras

Cheerful screams and flirtatious waves from the scantily dressed group of women paradegoers that passed by caused Jackson to smile. The cool night air was perfect for the late outdoor seating at the neighborhood creole cafe. The dining crowd for the evening was sparse with plenty of tables to choose from with the add benefit of no eavesdroppers.

A full day had passed, and I was still no closer to coming up with a plan to kill the lycanthrope taunting us and murdering others. The past week's events consumed my thoughts and left little room for anything other than putting out the proverbial personal fires that kept popping up.

A few blocks away, the masses screamed and raised their hands in a plea to be showered with plastic gifts from the costumed gods on the parade floats as they passed.

Tonight, I took the time to assemble the team to develop a

plan to identify and kill the most recent terror in the city. Ever since Goliath, New Orleans and its surrounding areas had been the city that endured one horror after another upon its citizens.

"Jackson, do I need to send a quick invite to Chloe to dine with us?" I asked with a smile.

"Let's not get snitchy here, Auntie. Just having a little fun. Nothing wrong with flirting, right?" Jackson replied. He responded with his own bright smile and added a playful wink.

Charles' brow curled, and I turned my head away from them both with a hand covering my grin. Somehow, I knew he was alluding to Jordan and me.

I supposed I wasn't as subtle as I thought with the playful banter with Jordan.

Considering what happened a few days ago, I'll have to come clean with Charles. I'm not comfortable lying to him. Although, it doesn't seem to be much of a problem for him.

After about an hour or so, the yells from the crowd in the distance became more prominent. The cloud covered sky functioned as a calming blanket as everyone quietly finished their meals and drinks. The unusual silence at the dinner table left what could only be described as a dejected atmosphere. For me, there was no doubt it was because of the lack of solutions to our current werewolf problem. We were all out of ideas. This was new territory for us.

Jordan decided not to join us and kept his nose in books to find a solution. Although, I assumed part of his decision to stay behind had something to do with sitting at the same table as Charles.

Tammy and Jackson both sat at the table with their heads

down. The bright light from their phone screens reflected off of their faces as both indulged in video games. Charles stared at me with a tension in his forehead, as if he desperately wanted to say something, but he couldn't find either the words or the courage to do so. It was as if they were waiting for me to provide the plan on how to put an end to this. I was out of answers.

"Maybe this wasn't such a good idea? We should put ourselves on lockdown until we have some sort of idea how to handle this. I can call City Hall and advise them to do the same. They should be receptive after losing their monster task force," I said. My eyes darted from one person to the other as I searched for a reaction.

"I knew deep down you were nothing but a scared little girl. All that pain from your childhood. All that trauma as an adult. It was obvious." The familiar voice asserted itself from the sidewalk area on the other side of the red-and-white striped rope that separated the outdoor table area from the walkway.

Charles turned his head in the person's direction. "Frank? What the hell are you doing here and why do you sound like that?" Charles asked.

"I'm here to see Nola." Frank smirked as he glared at me. His eyes were empty and soulless. "I didn't want to call. I figured this was a conversation we should have in person."

The guttural tone to his voice was eerie. Something about it was primal and familiar. I had heard it many times over the phone the past few years.

With widened eyes, I rushed to my feet, my attention fixed on Frank and his familiar tone. The rapid thump of my heartbeat pulsated in my ears.

"This is so sweet, having you all here together. Do you know how long I've waited to have you all together again? I've been so patient since the night I feasted on your old, withered neighbors' heart. I usually wouldn't bother with someone so aged. The taste of the heart of someone with so much wear and tear can be a bit bitter."

Charles sprang from his seat and vaulted over the rope. I immediately followed. Jackson and Tammy, now focused on what was going on in front of them, stood.

"Now, now, Charles . . . " Frank extended his palm in Charles' direction. His eyes lingered on Charles as he stepped closer. Frank's tensed jawline flexed as he appeared to grind his teeth. "Poor choice. Frank swung the back of his hand. He struck Charles across the face and propelled him upwards.

Charles soared a dozen or so feet in the air before he struck the base of a light pole. A sound rang out from the hollow pole as his head slammed against it. His body fell to the pavement, unconscious. Frank rotated his shoulders and head in a circular motion. The unusually loud crunch of his bones snapping filled the night's air. Frank screamed. His voice contorted into a deep, visceral growl. The bones in his face buckled. His skin appeared to boil as his features expanded and grew. Frank's eyes glowed a burning red. His body stretched, muscles swelled, and mutated as coarse gray hair sprouted from his skin.

I stood with my hand on the butt of Corbin, nestled in its shoulder holster. Frozen at the sight of the change that happened in front of me. I had hunted and killed dozens of lycanthropes before. Never had I ever seen one change right before my eyes. The lycanthrope changed aggressively and violently, yet with control, as if it had done so hundreds of times before. The heat and stench from its breath brushed against my face from its seven-foot frame as it growled.

It lunged toward me. Razor-sharp claws and skull-crushing size canine teeth hungry for flesh were now above me and burrowed down in my direction.

I panicked at the thought of something happening to Jackson. I could only think about Jackson. Instinct took over. Freed from its holster, my hands trembled as I took aim with Corbin. My feet became tangled in my rush to avoid its massive claws and teeth. I fell to the pavement.

Jackson pulled Guardian from his belt holster and extended the blade. The beast, swift in its motion, hurried past me. It struck Jackson in the chest with an open hand, extended its other, and wrapped its claws around Tammy's throat.

Jackson tumbled to the ground end over end. A low grumble of a laugh emanated from the monster. My eyes expanded at the sight of the terror on Tammy's face. Her arms and hands swung relentlessly as she struck the creature's beastly frame. Tammy pulled and wiggled to get free from its grasp.

I quickly raised Corbin and fired a few shots. The rounds ripped through its fur covered flesh.

The beast again laughed. "Succulent." It spoke in a low, gravelly voice.

It raised its claws and sliced through Tammy's chest. Blood spewed from her mouth. The beast tossed chunks of flesh and bone to the ground and tore out Tammy's heart with the same blood-soaked claws. The heart kept beating a few more times, spewing out blood from its open vessels. It bit into the heart. The warm, crimson colored liquid poured from the beast's mouth as its teeth tore through the tough muscle of her heart. Tammy's body went limp.

My eyes locked onto Jackson as he sat frozen at the sight of Tammy's flaccid body.

"No!" I yelled, expending the last few rounds from Corbin ineffectively into the lycanthrope.

Another bloodcurdling scream nearby echoed in the night. Tears fell from Charles' eyes, and his face filled with rage as he watched Tammy's body was on the pavement, unmoving. The pain that emanated from his scream cut through me. I winced at the piercing sound. The scream became distorted and cracked as it turned into a resonant growl.

I watched, incredulous, as the face of the man I loved became distorted. Massive teeth protruded from his mouth as his bottom facial features extended into a snout. The change was rapid and controlled, like Frank's before him. The disturbing sound of his bones as they reshaped was that of nightmares. Charles' eyes glowed a bright red as he howled toward the sky. What was once Charles growled in rage at the other werewolf that stood before him. Both were much larger than the other werewolves I had seen. Corbin fell from my hand and onto the ground.

"Oh my God," Jackson said, his voice just above a whisper as he turned and stared at me. Tears fell from his eyes.

Charles raced toward Frank and sliced through his gray fur with his claws. Blood gushed from his chest as Frank screamed with a high-pitched growl of agony. The two beasts entangled as they tore and ripped through each other with their claws and teeth. The beastly frames slammed against nearby cars, bending the frames and smashing the windows. Frank grabbed Charles by the throat and tossed him through the glass plate window of the restaurant where we sat and ate just a few minutes ago. Hands trembling, I picked up Corbin from the ground and attempted to reload it with more silver bullets with the speed loader strapped to my belt. The metallic smell of Tammy's blood filled my nose. Crippling nausea ravaged the pit of my stomach as I vomited. It was all too much.

This can't be happening.

Blood still dripping from his teeth, Frank grinned, and ran into the cover of the night.

Jackson ran to my side as I finished reloading Corbin, Guardian in hand. He froze at the sight of Tammy as she laid lifeless so close to him.

Charles' massive frame was taller than the height of the window he was just thrown through. As he stepped outside, my hands still trembled. My tears blurred the sight of him. Sharp, stabbing pains in my stomach caused me to bend over. I fought to stay upright and take aim with Corbin.

Charles' beastly form was familiar. His size, his black fur, and sharp teeth rivaled that of Frank and one other werewolf I had seen before. I struggled to wipe the tears away as I tried to get a clear look at him. He stared back at us. The tears from my eyes fell and slid into the deep crevice of the scar carved into my cheek. I reached to wipe it away.

The touch of the scar and the sight of Charles inundated my head with images of that night. The night I lost my parents. Murdered in the comfort of their home and in their bed. The night a massive, and nasty werewolf put this scar on my face and toyed with my life. A werewolf that I would recognize anywhere. One I had hunted for years. A werewolf that now stood in front of me once again.

The night fell silent. Only the rapid thumping of my

pounding heart filled my ears. The sound of my own rage-consumed scream filled my ears. Corbin violently shook in my hand as I lifted it. The rapid pull of the trigger was natural as my head filled with rage. Charles' beastly glare lingered as he watched me fire upon him without caution. He bared his teeth and uttered a low menacing sound as he fled, like Frank, into the cover of the night.

CHAPTER
SEVENTEEN

"LET'S NOT GET CONFUSED. YOU CAN'T KILL ME. IF YOU WANT TO TALK, WE CAN." — FRANK

"I suppose the time for secrets is over?" Frank grinned. The not-so-subtle hint of pride lingered on his face as he stepped to the side and allowed Charles inside. There was no need for theatrics. The crutch and the blood-soaked bandage were gone, along with Frank's limp.

Charles took only a few steps inside the hotel room and pivoted toward Frank, grabbing the fabric of his shirt and pinning him against the wall. Tears fell from Charles' eyes, brow tensed and contorted. His pupils burned a fire red. Charles drew a sharp breath.

"I'm going to kill you," Charles whispered, his lips pressed against Frank's ear and his eyes closed. "But first, I need answers."

Frank's once silent chuckle grew into an obnoxious laughter.

Charles' grip tightened. "Why did you murder Tammy?"

"She was pretentious and needed to be put in her place.

Just like that bitch girlfriend of yours. That'll happen in due time," Frank replied.

Charles pulled Frank from the wall and slammed him back, pinning him once again as Charles' knuckles whitened from the grip. The drywall cratered from the impact, and Frank's laughter continued.

"That's gonna cost you. Not yet, though. I have one more question. Are you my father? Whatever you do, don't lie to me." Charles pressed his tightly clenched fist against Frank's throat and pushed.

Frank continued to grin. Slumping his shoulders, his breath remained steady. His hand clutched Charles' throat and hoisted him. His feet kicked as he tried to get them back on the floor. Charles' grip loosened as Frank dropped him.

"Let's not get confused. You can't kill me. If you want to talk, we can." Frank adjusted his shirt near the collar and walked to the nearby chair in the corner and sat.

Charles picked himself up. His face still aimed toward the thick carpet of the hotel room floor as he wiped the tears from his eyes. He sat across from Frank. His skin brushed against the coarse fabric of the sofa as his shoulders shifted in search of comfort. Charles' fingertips turned pale as he gripped the edge of the sofa's armrest. His brow furrowed at the sight of Frank. The familiar musky smell of Frank's beastly side was now apparent to Charles somehow.

"Obviously, you have heightened senses. We've been around each other quite often these past few months. Do you know who I am?" Frank asked. His voice was barely above a whisper.

"Yes. Your scent had an allure, and I wasn't sure why. I didn't pick up on what you are or who you are, for certain. It always seemed something was masking your scent, as if you were wearing too much cologne. That was until you showed up last night. Then I knew you were my father," Charles replied

One corner of Frank's mouth lifted. His pride was apparent in his still hungry eyes. Frank walked over to the bar and poured an amber colored liquid into two glasses. The rest of the bottle made the trip back with Frank as he gave one glass to Charles. Both drank all the whiskey in their respective glasses with one swallow.

"I hid myself from you, just as I changed my voice with all those phone calls to Nola. Just one of the many talents you'll acquire the longer you live." Frank grinned and poured himself another glass. "Charles, we have a lot to talk about. I would like for you to keep your composure so we can get through this. After that, we can take this in any direction you wish. Although, I have a direction I would prefer. Understood?" Frank asked.

Charles glared at him, slamming the empty glass down on the nearby glass table next to the couch. His fingers repeatedly tapped the arm of the sofa. "No promises, asshole."

"Pissed about Tammy, right? She was too familiar. I don't take disrespect from children. I'm too old for that." Frank sat down again with his glass in hand. "That's what she was to me. That's what all of you are to me... children. It was going to happen, anyway. I'll kill everyone in your makeshift family and bring you home to us, your proper family. I want you to help me do it." Frank's grin was cold and matched the stillness in the depths of his eyes. The calm tone he spoke with reflected the remorseless and empty expression on his face. "The taste of a heart that has a love for you is the sweetest. When you devour it, it carries an essence of pleasure when you devour it that is unrivaled. You can't do what I can do yet. You're not old enough, but when you are, I can show you. We can indulge in their screams together, father and son."

Charles was still. His eyes locked on Frank. His mouth watered at Frank's description and the hunger he had spent years attempting to tame made its presence.

Charles exhaled sharply. "I'd rip out your heart first before I kill any of them. Besides, I plan to kill you because of what you did to her." His eyes never averted from Frank.

Frank rolled his eyes at Charles' theatrics. "I've kept my eyes on you all these years, Charles. Let's not act like you're not the animal you showed everyone last night. You hunt, kill, and feed on the flesh of human cattle to this day. You suppress your nature daily while you're around them. For what? All for a woman? A woman whose parents you murdered. You once hated her, as I do now, for killing so many of our kind. So, you hunted her. You found her parents and you killed them to inflict as much pain on her as you could. It was brilliant and beautiful. That is, until it became personal in Dalyville with your mother," Frank said.

"Nola helped me kill the creature that took my mother's likeness. When I needed her, she was there. She helped me through a tough time. I realized that killing everything and everyone in that town wouldn't have fixed it all. She showed me another way, and I love her for it. Jackson has given me the opportunity to be the father I never had. To be a father figure like you never wanted to be. I have the chance to be better than you. I am better than you. That's what I want."

Charles stood as he watched Frank's face sour from his words. He moved toward the large glass windowpane and pushed open the curtain. The hotel room's view looked down on the bustling tourist crowd packed together on Bourbon Street. The view mimicked that of ants rustling around on an ant farm.

Frank poured another glass of whiskey and swallowed. "Your mother raised a fool." Frank looked up from the bottom of his glass and glared at Charles. "That's not what you are. You're a lycanthrope. A special one. A hunter. The offspring of The First. You cannot suppress what you are, not for long, and you can't go back. Nola saw what you are tonight, and by now, I'm sure she's put together who you are and what you did. She will kill you, or at least die trying. The life you want is a delusion. Feed your hunger, and let's make this city our den. Charles, you aren't alone. You never were. You have a sister."

"Sister?" Charles asked. His voice raised slightly as he pivoted his head.

Frank laughed. He squeezed the bridge of his nose and shook his head in disbelief. "You can't possibly be this dense. Have you never wondered why you were different from the others? Did you do any research to understand what you are and why you're so strong?"

Charles' brow curled as he tried to find the words to answer.

"My mother was human. She told me a little about you. I recently open a letter she left for me upon her death. It warned me not to look for you. To forget about you. It wasn't until my twenties, while serving in the army, that I changed for the first time. I kept it from her. I kept it from Tammy as well. Everything I learned about werewolves only confused me more when I realized all the rules that were out there didn't apply to me. The silver, the moon cycle, my size and strength . . . and I don't remember ever being bitten. That's when I started to wonder who you were."

"You were never bitten by anything. You were born, like any other child." Frank's stare softened. "I never told your mother what or who I was. She only knew me as Frank, a real estate developer. She knew I had a keen business sense and that I enjoyed spending time with her. That's why she couldn't share anything about me. Your mother was unaware of what I was."

Charles took a few steps toward Frank, but he hesitated to get too close. He rubbed his hands together as he gathered his words again. "So, you did love my mother. You kept everything from her to protect her? You left to protect both of us from what you are?"

Frank laughed obnoxiously. "Absolutely not. I can't love a human. They're nothing but food, or a vessel if I choose to spread my seed. I enjoyed looking at her face. It pleased me. She pleased me. Ashley had some other traits I also enjoyed. It's why I chose her to carry you." Frank grinned and took a couple of steps closer to Charles. "I was confident she would take good care of you. I waited until you were born, then I left. Once the change happened, I knew I'd return for you. It was Dalyville and your irrational love for Nola Maor that I didn't see coming. Everything was much easier with your sister. I stayed in her life."

Charles clenched his right hand and threw a punch at Frank. Frank effortlessly stepped to the side and avoided it. The force of the punch knocked Charles to the floor. His eyes glowed red, and his brow and lips curled as he lay on the floor.

Frank's foot now rested upon the small of Charles' back. "You carry my blood. Your sister carries my blood. There are no others. She has accepted who she is and understands what's needed. She wants you on board. We both do." Frank lifted his foot off of Charles' back and let him up from the floor.

Charles brushed away any imaginary dust he might have seen with his hands as he stood. "Where's this sister of mine? Why isn't she here if I'm so important to you and to her?"

Frank once again laughed at Charles. The short, repetitive tones of his laugh provoked Charles' irritation.

"You really are dense. Tara stayed back in Europe. Just in case things went south here. It was unlikely, but I wanted to make sure someone was here to follow through with my desires." Frank replied.

"Oh, yeah. What are your desires?" Charles flopped his body back down onto the sofa. His sarcastic tone was loud. "What the fuck are you?"

"I am the first. You and your sister are born with my blood. That makes us the only three of our kind," Frank responded with a smile.

"Yeah, you said that already. I don't know what the hell that means, but you calling yourself 'The First' just because you have a dick and can impregnate a woman doesn't make you a god," Charles replied, unimpressed.

"I'm not a god. I'm telling you I am Prime. The true Alpha. The First of our kind, or whatever other name you want to put to it. All have come from me, through either the bite or through conception."

"What? How? If you're the first, then when were you born? How are you still alive?" Charles asked, tripping over his own words. He sat closer to the edge of the sofa.

"So impatient. One question at a time, child. I'll tell you everything." Frank poured himself another glass of whiskey. His words never slurred, and his movements never wavered. It didn't appear alcohol had much effect on him. "Have you ever heard of the tale of Saint Francis of Assisi and the wolf of Gubbio?"

Charles shook his head. His pupils moved to the upper left corner as if he was trying to pull the tale from memory.

"You should know your history, son. That knowledge is power. We probably wouldn't be having this discussion if you did."

"Don't call me, son. We haven't gotten there yet," Charles replied.

Frank's grin became apparent again. His eyes, however, remained absent any of reflection of humanity. "Centuries ago, I was human. I lived a holy life, and people in the surrounding villages knew me for helping others. I taught others how to farm, hunt, and even defend themselves. I longed for a life of servitude, praying that others would understand and accept my intentions. Not long after, a neighboring, gated town came calling for me. The people of Assisi had received word about a terribly enormous wolf was terrorizing the town of Gubbio. Livestock, townspeople, and even soldiers sent to kill it had fallen prey to the wolf. The town had all but shut down. People were afraid to leave their homes. So, they sent one brave soul beyond the gates to ask for my help." Frank said.

"You were a holy man?" Charles asked with his brow raised.

"Once. A very long time ago," Frank replied, nodding his head. "Because my fellow men needed me, I went to the town and eventually encountered the wolf. The town cowered in fear of the wolf by the time I arrived. Crops were dying, and the people were on the brink of starvation. It took only a couple of days, but eventually, I encountered the beast outside the town's walls. Red-eyed, the wolf towered over me, its height matching my shoulders. I had never seen a wolf like it."

"Why would the leadership of a town want a holy man to deal with wolf attacks?" Charles interrupted.

Frank smiled at Charles. "It was a different time back then, and I had a way with animals. A way that allowed me to calm them. That, along with the other skills I had, made me of value to others. There were plenty of others, including myself, who believed God protected me. They all believed I could compel the animal to leave the town in peace. When I saw this thing, it was beautiful. I knew there was something more to it. Not just its eyes and size, but it emanated this power, something otherworldly. I didn't fear it. I was envious of it. It was unlike anything I had ever felt before. Not in all my prayers and in all my attempts to get closer to God did I feel such a connection. It was as if it was waiting for me all this time. Much different from me seeking the power and presence of God. This wolf wasn't hiding in the darkness."

Frank's breathing became erratic as he rubbed the back of his neck. The color of his pupils turned hazel, and the whites of his eyes became bloodshot red. Frank inhaled deeply and tried to compose himself. The color of Frank's eyes reverted to the cold blue shade as his breathing stabilized.

"Do we have a problem?" Charles asked.

"Apologies. The thought of that moment sometimes pushes me to—Anyway, I needed to get closer. The beast growled and bared its massive teeth. A warning against my obvious desires to touch it. Something compelled me to reach out. I had to touch it. The intense heat it radiated felt as if it would fill the cold, dark place inside me. A lingering void despite my prayers. The sight and rhythmic sound of its teeth as they snapped at the air on my approach was hypnotic. In a primal way, the wolf spoke to me. The most savage parts of me found its essence intoxicating. I was close enough to feel the warmth of its breath upon my arm. It sunk its teeth into the flesh of my forearm. All I felt was bitter cold, and images of blood filled my head. I felt connected to it, and then fell unconscious," Frank said.

"Is that it?" Charles asked.

"When I woke up, the wolf was gone. There was no wound on my forearm, and I didn't feel any pain. At first, I thought it was a hallucination, until the people of Gubbio greeted me. They had smiles upon their faces and not a fearful look among them. They helped me up and thanked me for scaring off the beast. I will never forget the joy, hope, and the gratitude on their faces." Frank grinned and inhaled slowly. His eyes were closed, and his head leaned back slightly as he embraced the memory of that day. "To see those smiles . . . the rosy color of their faces and to hear the thump of their heartbeats surrounding me. Well, let's just say there's nothing more powerful than that first hunger."

"No . . . No. You didn't do what I think you did?" Charles asked. His eyes widened as he listened to Frank.

"I had no idea what was happening to me. The change was engulfing. I had never felt so powerful in the previous pathetic, insignificant life I lived. I killed, and I fed. When I was done, the entire town was dead— every man, woman, and child," Frank said. The smile on his face suggested nothing but pure satisfaction with himself as he fell silent.

"So, you've been like this for centuries?" Charles asked, his tone somber.

"Yes. We're immortal. Your sister was born before the new world was founded. The older we get, the stronger we get. Over time, we've acquired more abilities—being impervious to silver, changing at will, increased strength and size, the ability to hide our scent from others, and my favorite, total loss of humanity. Free to feed and live like the superior beings we are. Without the weight of empathy or remorse," Frank replied.

Charles stood and walked over to Frank. He placed his hand on Frank's shoulder with a look of concern. "Frank, thank you so much for the history lesson. For most of my life, I've struggled with what I was and where I came from. Things make so much more sense now."

"I'm glad you see where you belong, son. We're your family, not that pathetic excuse for flesh that you shacked up with. You are at a point in your blood life that your aging will begin to slow. She will notice. You are at your most powerful if you let go and allow the beast to take over for a while. That means letting go of the worldly connections and focusing on your hunt and your feed. It won't last forever, but your sister and I will be there to guide you through it. Let's take New Orleans for ourselves and make it our wolf's den," Frank replied.

The smile on Charles' face brightened as he gazed upon his father. "All I ever wanted was to find you and be a part of your life."

The nails on the hand near his side lengthened. The gruesome, black, razor-sharp nails ripped through Charles' flesh and hardened like steel as they extended. Charles quickly took a step back, striking Frank across the throat with his claws. Blood spewed from Frank's throat. Chunks of flesh were flung across the room and splattered against the ivory wall. Frank's eyes enlarged as he clutched his neck, attempting to stop the escape of his warm blood. His eyes fell closed as his limp body hit the hotel room floor.

"Get your ass up. I know it's not that easy," Charles said. Blood dripped from his nails as he walked to the door. "You took someone I loved. Now you want to take the only family I have left. I don't know how to kill you, but I'm sure we'll figure it out. When I see you again, I'm going to end you, and I'll do it in the most painful and vicious way possible. You deserve the torment, even if it's only a taste of the suffering and pain you've caused."

Frank stood as the wound on his neck mended. His voice returned "You made your choice. You'll see me soon, son." His grin returned. "Charles, tell Nola that I'm here to collect, and I'll see her soon as well. I'm sure her heart will taste delightful."

Charles turned his back on Frank and walked out the door. Not another word was spoken.

CHAPTER
EIGHTEEN

"IT KILLED HER. IT KILLED TAMMY. I SAW THEM PUT HER IN THAT CORONER'S VAN." — JACKSON

Monday (Lundi Gras)—One day before Mardi Gras

A gentle cool breeze caressed the air that night. One of the many benefits of an early Mardi Gras for the tourists and New Orleans natives. For the past few years, it seemed New Orleans could count on either cold or rainy weather on Fat Tuesday. The cool air paired well with the crowd's indulgence in the satisfying burn of premium alcohol. People passed, sipping from plastic cups, as I watched. I got it. I used to enjoy that burn. Now I just wanted a quiet place to think after everything that had happened. I wasn't expecting the paradegoers to spill over into the Parish Park area.

I wasn't in the mood to tolerate the debauchery. This was probably a bad idea. The cold metal from the park bench, the fallen leaves from the towering trees above, and the rustling of the branches as the wind sliced through them—it was all too familiar. I thought revisiting the place where I almost met my demise at the vicious claws of Goliath might help me remember the pain and desperation I felt when I thought I was about to die.

There was no pain, only rage. Betrayal didn't cover what I felt. Under the same roof, lying in the same bed, sharing each other's bodies and thoughts. I ate at the same table with the monster that killed my parents. I screamed into the night as rage spilled out of me. The glares from intoxicated pedestrians that were still partying in the park encouraged them to mimic my screams to turn the calm atmosphere into a late-night party environment. They had no idea how dangerous this city was about to get.

"What the hell, people? This is a family park, and it's damn near 3 a.m. Don't any of you go home, for Christ's sake?" I yelled. My scream remained largely ignored.

Jackson sat next to me. His shoulders slumped, and his eyes welled with tears. His leg quivered as he stared off into the distance. "It killed her. It killed Tammy. I saw them put her in that coroner's van. She's gone. She's really gone," Jackson mumbled. Tears fell as he stood, his face creased in worry. I watched as his dismay turned to rage. "And Charles! I told you there was something off about him. How could you miss that?" Jackson yelled.

"I—I don't know. What we had blinded me, I suppose. I lost everyone. Guess I could only see what I needed." Standing, I wiped the tears away from Jackson's face. "I should have seen it. Charles was back on his feet way too fast from those banshee wounds in Dalyville. All the trips back and forth to New York for business were probably just cover stories when he wanted to feed. This is my fault. I was only thinking about what I wanted. Consumed by what I needed."

Since the loss of his parents, I hadn't noticed the pain that lingered in Jackson's eyes. I never thought I would see him in that type of pain again. I let him down.

The sparse crowd that lingered inside the park turned up the volume on the portable radio that accompanied them. The festive sound of the seasonal Mardi Gras song led me to roll my eyes and scoff. A few shots from Corbin into that piece of shit radio would not only solve the problem of the music, but it would also get rid of these jerks who apparently didn't have to worry about work in the morning. Neither the music nor the people seemed to bother Jackson one bit. He hadn't taken his tear-filled glare off of me since I stood in front of him.

"Auntie Nola, Tammy is dead! There's a nasty lycanthrope hunting us, and the one that killed my grandparents has been living under our roof for almost four damn years. What are we going to do? We still don't know what kind of lycanthrope they are," Jackson said, his voice wavering.

A lump formed in my throat, hindering my ability to swallow upon hearing the pain in Jackson's voice. That fear, which hadn't filled me since the night my parents were murdered, gripped me. I had no words to comfort him.

"His name is Saint Francis of Assisi, and he's my father." The voice emerged from the shadows behind me. An unrelenting chill accompanied the breeze as the trees swayed above. Charles stood tall as he stared at both me and Jackson. The shadows of the night partially covered him in a dark silhouette. The subtle, enticing fragrance of his cologne carried in the breeze. His scent triggered brief memories of pleasant past intimate encounters. "He claims to be the first lycanthrope. Born of some sort of wolf deity. Frank also claims to be immortal. I have more that I can share," Charles said as he carefully took a step forward. "I just want to—"

A single gunshot echoed into the night's air. The crowd scattered in panic and confusion. Their screams carried as they ran out of the park. A trickle of smoke rose from the onyx tip of the barrel of Corbin.

Charles's body fell limp and smacked against the chilly blades of grass and dried leaves of the park. Blood trickled from the quarter-sized wound in his forehead, yet spilled from the gaping exit wound in the back of his head. Charles' eyes were lifeless. I holstered Corbin, its barrel still smoking.

Jackson stared at me in shock as he watched my actions. His brow raised and openmouthed. "Do you think he's dead?" Jackson asked.

"I hope so. He was in his human form. Whatever the case, we can't wait around here to find out. What these people just witnessed . . . they'll believe it was a murder. We have to get out of here," I said. I wiped a tear away.

Jackson spat upon Charles' body as we walked by.

"Let's go, Jackson. We should get some rest. There's a prime lycanthrope to kill."

CHAPTER NINETEEN

"JACKSON, BEHIND YOU!" — CHLOE

The next morning, Jackson awakened in a cold sweat from a nightmare. The images of the blood-covered teeth of Frank and Charles impelled him to spring out of bed, grab his cell phone and run to the door. Still in the blue jeans and university T-shirt he wore last night before he passed out on his bed, Jackson felt the exhaustion hit him before he made it to the door.

Yesterday felt like a dream, or more accurately, a nightmare. Visions of Tammy as blood spilled from her mouth clouded Jackson's mind. He stumbled and fell onto the grass of the front lawn. Jackson made his way back to his feet and into his truck. Foot on the accelerator, white smoke spewed from under the rubber of the spinning tires as he sped away. Jackson yelled into the speaker of his cell phone. "Call Chloe!"

The phone rang a few times. His heart raced as he drove.

How could I have been so stupid? I can't believe I forgot to warn her. God, if anything happens to her . . .

"Hey, baby. I was just think—"

"Chloe, listen to me. Where are you?" Jackson yelled into the cell phone speaker.

Chloe stopped and pulled the phone momentarily from her ear. Jackson had never called her in a panic before. "I'm walking back from the library on campus, headed back to the dorm. I'm pretty tired. I've been at it all night. Where have you been?"

"Stop! Listen! Get back to the dorm now. I need you to run. We found out who that werewolf is, and it's coming for all of us. We don't know how to kill it, and it's strong . . . really strong. Charles is one too. Or . . . maybe was one. We don't know," Jackson blurted, almost incoherent as the words spilled from him.

"Wait, what? Charles is a *what*?" Chloe stopped walking along the sidewalk. Her eyes widened. She watched as Jackson quickly parked the truck and jumped out.

"I'm on campus, and I'm not far from you. It showed itself to us last night. It killed Tammy. She's dead." Jackson's voice cracked on the other end of the phone. His heavy breathing was apparent. "There you are. I see you. Run toward me."

Jackson stood on the other end of the sidewalk near the road as the early morning sun reflected off the blade of the Guardian as he waved it back and forth.

Chloe clutched the straps of her backpack and ran toward Jackson. Her stride shortened as her vision cleared from the blinding reflection of light from Guardian. A scream of terror echoed through the empty courtyard as Chloe spotted the enormous creature lurking near Jackson. Its gray fur and oversized teeth were a terrifying and unexpected sight. Somehow, the creature was even more horrifying in daylight than under the cover of darkness the night it had killed Mrs. Bradley.

"Jackson, behind you!" Chloe yelled, still running toward him.

The wolf lunged at Jackson as he fell to the ground, heeding Chloe's warning. Its massive sprawling body flew through the air. Its sharp claws attempted to rip through Jackson as he rolled away, putting distance between himself and the beast.

Jackson made his way to his feet with him and Chloe standing on each side of the creature. It turned to Jackson and grinned. A hunger for blood was apparent in the menacing expression of its bloodred eyes. With a broader, more ravenous grin, the monster turned toward Chloe. The growl that emanated from it was subtle.

"Chloe, get to the truck," Jackson yelled as he maneuvered toward the beast. "Frank!"

He closed the distance between himself and the werewolf in a matter of moments. The beast tried to make its way to Chloe. Jackson leaped in the air, plunging the full length of Guardian into its fur covered back. The werewolf screamed in agony. Its body jerked in pain. Its claws reached back, hoping to remove the blade that now protruded through its chest. Jackson grabbed hold of the handle of Guardian. He depressed the button on the handle, retracting the silver blade. The blood of the wolf sprayed onto his face as he fell to the ground. The beast clawed at its chest. It swung its beastly arm around in a panic. The werewolf's backhand struck Jackson on the shoulder, which sent him tumbling to the ground. Jackson quickly sat up, reached for Chloe's hand, already extended down toward him.

Chloe pulled Jackson to his feet. They sprinted to his truck past the four other vehicles that were parked in front of the university. Chloe heard the sound of the beast's angry howl in the distance. Chloe and Jackson jumped in the truck and sped off with Chloe in the passenger's seat.

Sweat dripped from Chloe's brow. Jackson wiped the blood from his eyes as it obstructed his vision, smearing it across his face. Chloe had never seen Jackson's face covered in fear. Her heart pounded violently at the sight of Jackson's labored breaths and wide eyes; his face stained in the creature's blood.

"Pull out your phone and call my aunt," Jackson pleaded.

Chloe retrieved the cell phone from her pocket and hurriedly dialed. A loud thump came from the roof of the car. The top now slightly caved in. Jackson clutched the steering wheel with both hands, pressing down further on the gas pedal. The oversized pickup truck accelerated down the road. Its engine roared in the morning air.

Black claws penetrated the roof of the truck and sliced through the metal covering. The werewolf smashed the passenger side window as it reached in to grab hold of Chloe. Chloe screamed and leaned closer to Jackson. She jerked the steering wheel in a panic. The truck swerved from side to side as Jackson tried to regain control.

"Chloe, what the fuck was that?" Jackson yelled.

"I'm sorry. I'm sorry." Tears flowed from her eyes.

The voice on the other end of the phone answered.

"Hello."

"Nola, it's on the roof of the truck. It's ripping through. It's trying to kill us!" Chloe yelled. Her voice was shaky and filled with a deep, resonating fear that felt as if it was choking off her air supply.

She slid lower into the seat and enacted the Bluetooth option of the call as it connected to the truck. The razor-sharp claws continued to cut through the truck's roof, pulling back a small portion of the truck's rooftop. Not quite enough for it to slip its massive arm through. The brightness of the new morning sun, still low in the sky, partially obstructed both Chloe's and Jackson's view.

Jackson pressed his foot on the gas pedal a little more. The roar of the truck's engine groaned louder as they accelerated down the narrow neighborhood street that led downtown. Jackson swerved the truck from side to side, trying to shake off the beast. Its supernatural strength refused to be influenced by Jackson's attempt to lose it.

"Jackson, where are you?" Nola's panicked voice on the other end of the phone and speakers of the truck pleaded for an answer.

"I'm driving down Loyola Avenue. I'm about to cross Claiborne Avenue, headed toward the stadium," Jackson yelled back. The rumbles of the werewolf on top of his car were louder than he could yell.

Chloe quickly glanced up at the roof of the truck and saw the menacing red glow of the wolf's eyes staring back at her through the tattered holes in the roof.

"Listen, stay calm and get to the stadium. Whatever you do, don't slow down. Get into the stadium's parking garage. That building is fifty years old. The clearance height for modern trucks isn't there. Get there, now!" Nola yelled.

The werewolf continued to rip away at the roof of the truck, thrusting its snout and bloodthirsty canines into any hole it pried open. The jagged metal edges sliced at its flesh.

Jackson tossed a detracted Guardian into Chloe's lap. "When I tell you, hit the switch and extend the blade. Drive it through its fucking head. Then retract it," Jackson said, his voice in a high-pitched tone.

The sight of the giant domed stadium that emerged in front of them caused Jackson to accelerate. Chloe, still crouched down in her seat, closed her eyes and waited for Jackson's signal. The structure was so massive that it could only be obscured by the intricate twists and turns of the interstate ramps above them. The entrance to the parking garage of the stadium was fast approaching.

"Chloe, now!"

Chloe pressed the handle of Guardian up to the shredded roof of the truck and lined it up with the werewolf's eye as it peered inside. She depressed the button on the handle. Her arm jumped from the recoil as the machete blade penetrated the weakened roof of the truck and ripped through the werewolf's skull. Chloe depressed the button again and quickly retracted the blade. Blood spilled from the wound of the beast and covered her hair and face.

In front of them was the bright yellow, heavy pole which stretched across the two-lane entrance with '6 ft Clearance' stenciled across it. Jackson fully depressed the gas pedal to the floor of the truck, speeding toward the entrance. Sparks emitted from the undercarriage as Jackson's truck dipped slightly, passing under the clearance bar.

The heavy, high-density polyethylene tensile strength bar slammed into the werewolf, which caused a high-pitched tone like a mallet that struck a gong. Its claws ripped through the few remaining pieces of roof metal of the truck in a desperate attempt to hold on from the crushing impact. Its lacerated and twisted body hit the pavement as blood poured from under it. Jackson drove through the parking garage, then slowed after losing the lycanthrope.

"Jackson! Jackson, did you make it? Are you okay?" An antsy Nola yelled on the other end of the phone call; the speaker phone still engaged.

"We're good, Auntie. We lost it. Great plan," Jackson said as he inhaled and exhaled slowly to calm himself.

Chloe sat in the passenger seat, silent, with a distant look in her eyes, unable to provide herself or Jackson any comfort after such a close call. Her hands trembled as her fingers barely clutched the handle of Guardian. Her mouth moved timidly as she spoke.

"I—I'm here, Nola. We're good," Chloe said.

Nola sharply exhaled on the other end of the line. "Christ. Thank God. Okay, it's Lundi Gras morning. Get your asses over here before the streets flood with people. This isn't over. I doubt that iron bar did anything to hurt it. Keep Chloe close. Stay with her and protect her. I'll find Jordan. We'll meet tomorrow morning and figure something out."

"Agreed. We're on our way," Jackson said.

As Jackson and Chloe drove off, Frank's bones reassembled themselves. As the broken bones reassembled, the body crunched with violent torque. The gaping wound in his skull mended as he stood. The bones snapped and crunched as they healed. He howled toward the sun on the early Lundi Gras morning. Mardi Gras was always a time for celebration and a time to let loose and party. For Frank, it was a time to feast.

CHAPTER
TWENTY
"I GUESS YOU'RE ABOUT TO GET YOUR ANSWER, JORDAN." — NOLA

Mardi Gras Morning

The atmosphere inside the house wasn't the normal expectation for a Mardi Gras morning. What was usually a home filled with the sound of music playing, the aroma of a large pot of red beans and rice, some seafood étouffée, and imported beers iced down in an oversized cooler on Fat Tuesday morning, was now a quiet and somber environment. Curtains pulled closed, withdrawn faces, and a lack of any appealing aromas or sounds was a bit sobering.

They had rearranged the living room furniture to accommodate two large folding tables filled with a variety of specialty weapons from both the study and storage. Each weapon was designed to inflict a specific amount of damage on creatures of the occult without mercy.

"This is everything we have. If this were a normal werewolf, everything laid out on these tables would inflict some type of wound and would be more than capable of putting one down permanently. With Frank, we just don't know. But we better figure it out, and quickly," I said.

I observed the blank expressions on their faces as we surrounded the tables. Jackson and Jordan mulled over the items and weighed their options. With a blank expression on her face, Chloe stared at a nearby wall, her eyes fully open.

"Chloe. Chloe!" I yelled, snapping my fingers. She blinked rapidly as she shifted toward me. "I'm here. Just thinking," Chloe answered.

There was no way she was in any condition to face this thing again. The night with Mrs. Bradley was one thing, but Chloe's and Jackson's close call this morning might have been a little too much for her. It came as no surprise. Chloe was skilled, but still a novice with all of this. Frankly, I'd be concerned if she was unaffected by what happened. She had to be. We all were.

"Chloe, I want you here. You need to sit this one out."

"What? Nola, no. I can help," Chloe responded.

While polishing Guardian's blade with a mixture containing traces of silver and wolfsbane extract, Jackson continued to focus on the weaponry on the tables.

"I know you can. You're capable, but you just went through something yesterday, and it'll take more than one night's sleep to work through it. You need to continue to process it in a safe and calm environment. Trust me. This thing is hunting us. It attacked you on your campus ,and you won't be safe here at my place." I reached into my jean pocket and grabbed the set of keys inside. "I have a key to Mrs. Bradley's house. You can hide out next door until all of this blows over. You should be safe. Besides, Frank has his sights set on me, Jackson, and Jordan."

"Jackson, are you okay with this? I was just with you and

handled myself fine. You guys can use me," Chloe said. She stormed around the table to stand in front of Jackson, her cheeks void of color.

Jackson leaned in close to Chloe's ear. "She wants to protect you. It's in case this thing beats us. You would be the last hunter in the city," Jackson whispered. He kissed her gently on the cheek after.

Chloe peered up at me and quickly turned away as her eyes watered.

"Guys, I hate to interrupt, but where the hell is Charles?" Jordan asked.

I glared at Jordan and inhaled sharply, hesitating to answer. With everything that has happened, I didn't get the chance to give Jordan all the details of Tammy's murder, or that I put a bullet in that son of a bitch's head.

My cell phone on the table vibrated. The name displayed on the illuminated screen sent my heart pounding ferociously in my chest. I wasn't sure I would ever see that name light up on my phone again, and I hesitated as I answered the call.

"I guess you're about to get your answer, Jordan," I said before I pressed the green circle. "Charles, you're alive. I wasn't sure if that would work or not."

A quick glance at Jordan made evident the bewilderment plastered on his face.

"That was unnecessary. You knew that wouldn't kill me," Charles said.

I pressed the speaker phone option on the cell phone to allow everyone to listen. Charles' betrayal effects them all "I had no idea what would happen. You were in your human form. It was a silver bullet, and it went through that massive head of yours. I was hoping it would do the job and free you from all of those lies you keep caged inside there."

"Nola, I know I owe you the truth about everything, and I promise you I'll make this right. Just to get you up to speed, Frank is my father. I was born, not bitten. I know you're angry, but you can't mean those things. Despite everything, I always showed you who I was. What we have is real. You know me," Charles said, his voice soft.

Jordan sat in silence after hearing what Charles said. Jackson tapped the handle of Guardian on the table repeatedly at the sound of Charles' voice.

"Yeah, no shit, he's your father. I meant every word, asshole. Are you delusional? You think I can forget what you did to my parents because we shared a bed? You put this damn scar on my face. I've done nothing but dream about killing you for fifteen years. Now, not only will I get you, but I'll get to kill your piece of shit father as well. That sounds like justice to me," I said.

The phone fell silent for a few moments.

"Nola, I love you. If I could take it all back, I would. But I can't. I was different then. I hated that you were killing so many of my brothers and sisters, and I wanted you in pain. So, I hunted you down and took your parents. I put that scar on your face, so you would think of me daily. I didn't expect to run into you in Dalyville. That caught me by surprise. I planned on killing you then, but I saw another side of you. You showed so many people empathy there, and you helped me. I was a total stranger. You put all the pain you were going through aside. You helped me put down the cannibals that killed my mother and the monster that used her likeness. Something changed in me that night. I fell in love with you and saw my younger self in

Jackson. With everything he lost, all I wanted to do was be a father figure for him, a friend, something I never had."

Jackson's brow relaxed. The anger reflected in his face moments ago was gone. The voice on the other end of the phone was the man I fell in love with. My mind raced with thoughts of Charles and the happy moments we had shared over the past few years. My eyes watered, and I wiped the tears away from my cheek. The deep indentation of the scar that stretched the length of the left side of my face caused me to pull my hand away. I exhaled slowly as Charles continued to plead his case.

"Jackson. Jackson, I know you can hear me. I know I'm on speaker. I love you, Jackson. I could never replace your father, but I consider you my son. Look, I know we didn't always get along. I was still figuring things out. I'm still learning," Charles yelled.

"Why?" Jackson asked.

"Because I knew the pain of growing up without a father," Charles replied.

"No. Why have you lied all these years? You could have told us anytime. You chose to hide," Jackson said.

I glanced at Jackson. The scowl previously worn on his face reappeared.

"Jackson, I had . . . I'll prove it to both of you. Don't bother leaving the house. Just stay safe. I'll take care of this. I'll kill Frank."

The sound of two beeps immediately followed after Charles ended the call.

Jordan stared at me; one eyebrow raised. I knew what he was thinking. The room was once again silent. The array of weapons on the table was at odds with the expressions on the faces in front of me. Their expressions screamed *enough*. It was obvious that they all just wanted it to end. They wanted some peace. A chance to put this all behind them and enjoy life. Charles' offer was tempting. As tempting as any source of light in a time of darkness. My temptation was fleeting.

"Chloe, get your ass next door. Guys, grab what you think will be effective. Saint Charles Avenue will have the densest population for parades this morning. Let's fucking end this."

CHAPTER
TWENTY-ONE
"GUYS, I THINK HE'S HERE." — NOLA

The compactness of the festive crowd was business as usual for a Mardi Gras morning. The sky was a beautiful, clear, ocean blue. An array of bright green, purple, and yellow clothes adorned by parade goers, along with the same themed house decor, flooded every sightline as far as my eyes could see. Thousands of people stretched their arms and hands up high toward the decorated trailers as they screamed and pleaded for the beaded plastic blessings thrown to them by the drunken costumed gods on top of the carnival floats. Each float passed filled with riders with bags filled with assorted throws for the crowd. The scantily clad women used their best assets to garner the attention of the masked riders to reap the best rewards thrown in their direction. Short skirts showed off more than the law usually allow for both men and women alike.

Not today, though. Mardi Gras day allowed for the temporary suspension of some local laws. Today was about release.

Release from all the bullshit life had brought. Most chose to release it all by music and dance, or screams pleading to floats for rewards. Others drowned their problems with a steady flow of cocktails and Creole cuisine. Not too long ago, I would have been one of those people enjoying the sinful activities. All before I had to repent on the following day, Ash Wednesday, and satisfy my Catholic obligation.

The bass of the loud music from a radio that played nearby a group of parade goers infected me. I found myself nodding as I tapped my foot and enjoyed the sights of another illustrious Mardi Gras day. I stopped when I realized what was happening. We weren't here for that. Today could turn ugly if I let the festivities distract me.

The brick building behind me provided a solid wall to lean against to protect my own back and remove the chance of someone coming up from behind me. There were only three of us. Three hunters to cover and monitor dozens of blocks that made up a parade route. It was bad enough the constant movement of the people in the area was triggering my anxiety. The random screams from those people as they walked by with cocktails in hand that made it harder to maintain my focus. The constant turning of my head exhausted my neck. It was like watching several tennis matches all at once.

"Anyone see anything yet?" I struggled to hear my voice over the boisterous crowd when I spoke into the walkie-talkie.

"Nothing yet," Jackson replied from the other side of the street.

"Nola, are we sure Frank will try to make his move today and at this location? I mean Mardi Gras parades and festivities are all over the damn city. Why here? Not that I mind the premium seat to the titty show," Jordan said, staring down at me from the roof of a small building across the street from Jackson's position.

Jackson laughed into the walkie-talkie.

Glancing up at the rooftop, I could see the brightness of his smile from here. Jordan had been a rock-solid partner for me since he decided to leave the police department and join the team. Steady through every up and down I had, as well as every up and down this family has had. He was smart, strong, attractive, and funny. I wasn't a huge fan of his sarcasm and crass jokes, though. Quick flashes of thoughts of our moment together forced a smile on my face and a tingle down my spine.

"Look here, funny man. Focus on the task at hand. The titties can wait. Frank wants to gut this city. That means he needs to bite as many people as he can to build himself a den. He'll want to make a spectacle of it too. You can't get more high-profile than Mardi Gras day on St. Charles Avenue, especially with the number of people and media out here," I said as I smiled back at him. Somehow, I could see his eyes from here.

"Makes sense. You're pretty smart, boss lady," Jordan replied. His smile was still clearly visible from the distance.

"Guys, do I need to be the adult here? Keep your eyes open. And, when this is over ... get a room," Jackson said.

Damn it! He said the quiet part out loud. How does he know?

I quickly ducked as a bushel of plastic beads sped toward my head, thrown from the passing float. The beads smacked against the bricks and fell to the sidewalk. One of the float riders caught me slipping. They tended to throw them at anyone they caught not participating in their worship. A time-honored tradition like no other. Free concussions.

"Asshole."

Another massive super-float passed, carrying dozens of

costumed people with the soulful music of one of the inner-city school marching bands stepped behind it. The gyration and pageantry of the drum majors' performances were that of part soldiers and part dancers. The three students high-stepped and twirled their golden staffs in the air as the incredible one-hundred-person marching band played the soulful sounds of Earth, Wind, and Fire's "September" with volume and precision. Only in New Orleans did the band members often outshine the athletes in the high school hierarchy.

As I resisted the urge to get distracted by the performance of the band, I scanned the crowd and watched passively as everyone enjoyed the parade. Kids mounted onto their father's shoulders. A cluster of ladies danced together in a circle, arms in the air as they gyrated their hips. The women wore all-in-one catsuits with large, bold stripes in Mardi Gras colors. An outfit worn by many, regardless of their physical shape or size.

Beads of sweat clustered on my brow as the sun shone more prominently in the sky. A warm day for a Fat Tuesday that fell in February this year. Wearing a jacket today wasn't part of my plan, but guns along the parade route were a big violation. It didn't matter. There was no way I was going to confront anything without Corbin on my side. It's why I could only shake my head at the foolish man that stood in front of the dancing women in a full suit. A white suit, for that matter. Just the sight of him made me feel hotter than I already felt. The stillness of the man indicated he was unbothered by the rising temperature. He seemed unaffected by the music and the celebrations around him as well.

Moments passed. He hadn't moved, not one single inch. The sight of the back of his head covered with slick gray hair made it difficult to avert my eyes. I stepped away from the brick wall as my heart pumped faster. My breathing became slightly erratic.

I raised the walkie-talkie. "Guys, I think he's here," I said, walking a couple of steps closer to the dancing women.

Placing the walkie-talkie in my left hand, I reached with my other hand under my jacket and rested it comfortably on the butt of Corbin. The band started up with another song, drowning out any reply from Jackson or Jordan on the walkie-talkie. The man slowly turned around to face me, as if he already knew I was behind him. It was Frank. His unnatural and creepy grin was enough to darken the world around him. The look on his face differed from any other time I had seen him. Frank's eyes were empty, void of any humanity.

I pulled Corbin from my holster and ran toward Frank.

"GUN!" An on-looker in the mass of people yelled.

Screams and panic erupted from the crowd as they scattered in multiple directions at the sight of Corbin. The bright white suit worn by Frank was lost in the chaos. The once controlled party atmosphere was now a sight of panicked parade goers running in reaction to the warning.

"Does anyone have eyes on him?" I yelled into the speaker of the walkie-talkie.

I only received the crackle of a broken signal from the speaker in response. Unable to put my sights on Jackson or Jordan, I ran deeper into the crowd in search of the white suit.

As I cut through the chaos, person after person bumped into every side of me as they wormed their way in the other direction. Struggling to make my way through as if I was swimming in the thickness of oil, the bright reflection of the sun against Frank's gaudy white suit caught my attention. There he stood on the second-floor balcony of one of the many St.

Charles Street mansions, an unnaturally wide grin on his face. His hand firmly clutched the back of a woman's neck. She was in tears.

I raised the walkie-talkie in hopes of reaching Jordan, who already had a high position. More crackling.

It was too dangerous to take a shot. One mistake or one slightly misguided aim when I fired and someone could get hurt or, even worse, killed.

Frank's suit ripped away from his body. His frame violently contorted and stretched. Fur sprouted from his pores and covered his powerful body. Canine teeth reached with hunger from its mouth, and its claws wrapped around the neck of a nearby screaming woman. Frank's wolf form pulled the woman closer, and its teeth sank into the fleshy shoulder of his hostage. She screamed in agony as blood gushed from her. The wolf hungry eyes glared back at me with a blood-soaked grin, crimson colored flesh stuck between its teeth.

"Auntie Nola, I see it and I see you. On my way to you," Jackson said. His voice was finally clear over the speaker.

Brow furrowed, I squinted at what I saw. The beast released the woman and jumped on to the roof of the adjacent home. She fell to the balcony floor, screaming in pain. Frank was nowhere in sight.

My chest rose and fell rapidly as I tried to catch my breath at the sight of events that unfolded in front of me.

The grip I had on the walkie-talkie loosened at the thought of what could be coming. The pleasurable aroma of the still simmering barbecue grills along the parade route clashed with the thoughts of the expected bloodshed ahead. Jackson and Jordan ran toward me, along with dozens of uniformed police officers.

"Officers, there's a woman on that balcony that needs an ambulance," I said, watching as a few rushed to her to give aid.

"Nola, no guns on the parade route. That law applies to you too." The officer pointed his finger at me. His squinted. "What the hell am I saying? I saw that damned thing on the balcony. If the gun wouldn't have scared the crowd, it would have been a lot worse," the officer said.

I closed my eyes momentarily as I took a slow, deep breath. My eyes were now fixed on Jackson and Jordan. "I know what it wants. What Frank really wants." I holstered Corbin and secured the strap. "Yes, Frank wants us dead. All of us. But his long game isn't some real-estate monopoly of the city. It's something worse. Do you remember the werewolf attack at the cafe? Two patrons suffered injuries during the werewolf attack and were rushed to the hospital. "I didn't tell you that the werewolf bit them."

"That means . . . Where are they? They had to change by now. They had to feed on someone," Jordan said.

"They haven't. That night, I snuck into the hospital and killed them both before they could change. I didn't want to tell you that. I wanted to spare you, Jackson. It's not the way we do things. I couldn't let them change and take the chance of me not being there to stop them before they killed someone," I said.

Jackson and Jordan averted their eyes, obviously conflicted with my decision.

"Now we have another person bitten. His purpose wasn't to kill us or anyone else out here. He wanted to show me. He plans on infecting hundreds of citizens and making New Orleans his personal capital, eventually overwhelming us and killing us," I said.

Jordan stared at me and smiled with only the corner of his mouth. "Corrupting you in the process before he rips your heart out. He saw what you would do at that hospital and now he wants to continue his games. Un-fucking-believable, Nola," Jordan yelled, shaking his head and taking a couple of steps away in anger.

"Wait. Charles is still out there. He claims he wants his father dead, so what if Frank can convince Charles to work with him and choose his blood family?" Jordan asked.

"Game over," I replied.

The other uniformed officers stood around us and stared into the distance. Their eyes were vacant with fear. The Emergency Medical Services removed the woman from the balcony and put her in an ambulance. Thoughts of putting a bullet in her head right now came just as fast as they went.

"So, what do we do? If an area like St. Charles Avenue on Mardi Gras morning didn't facilitate the type of crowd he wanted, what would?" Jordan asked.

As I contemplated what would be Frank's next likely target, I watched the crowd start to re-gather along the parade route after the police gave the all-clear. New Orleans never gave up on its sacred holiday. Not until the clock struck midnight. When it hit me, my heart pace quickened at the thought of it.

"There's an area where the streets aren't this wide. The crowd would be twice as thick, with people packed shoulder to shoulder. Any chaos would only cause people to trip over themselves or others. There would literally be no place to run. He could maximize his carnage. Worse, if there are two or three of them, it would be a complete disaster," I said.

"Oh my God!" Jordan replied.

Jackson stared at us both with confusion. He wasn't a partygoer, so his lack of awareness didn't surprise me.

"What? Somebody say something," Jackson said.

"The place where most go for the final hours of Mardi Gras day and the home of any person's particular flavor of debauchery... Bourbon Street," I said.

CHAPTER
TWENTY-TWO

Mardi Gras Night—Bourbon Street.

Cold temperatures, nasty rainy weather, and muddy streets had burdened Mardi Gras the past few years. Not this year. A long overdue clear and beautiful day, which lasted into a perfect night, graced this year's Fat Tuesday. A night that displayed a bright three-quarter moon prominently in the sky. Under normal circumstances, that moon should have been a delay in the possible carnage that awaited. It didn't matter in this situation; these weren't normal circumstances. This werewolf didn't need a full moon. The beast within was in full control. It was the first, the prime. Even worse, there was another just like it somewhere in the city. The hunt for Charles had to wait another day.

The crowd was thick and boisterous down below. Thousands of heavily intoxicated people crammed together like chickens in a slaughterhouse. The amount of uninhibited half-naked people roaming around with drinks in their hands and plastic beads around their necks partying agitated my anxiety, with them so closely packed together. All the while, I remained envious of their ability to let go. For years, I hadn't allowed myself to let go and have fun. Although it wasn't that appealing to all the senses. Even from the roof of one of the smaller buildings on Bourbon Street, the odors of sweat, urine, and alcohol induced a mild sensation of nausea. Of course, I probably could have picked a better location to stake out than the roof of the topless and bottomless strip club.

Stretching thirteen blocks, Bourbon Street was a lot of ground to cover. Strategically, with only three of us, it made sense to keep our focus on the three most crowded blocks of tourists. The police department had a friendly presence, with a few officers posted on each block. Unfortunately, those officers weren't aware of what to look for and just how dangerous tonight would get.

"Are we sure this is it? I mean, there are parties all over the city. We can't be wrong about this," Jackson said. There was a hint of apprehension in his voice over the walkie-talkie.

"This is our best guess. I'd say it's a pretty damn good guess too. Just keep your eyes open. Whatever happens, watch where you fire. I saw you brought that crossbow, Jackson. Slow reload time, so make your shots count. That goes for you and Corbin too, Nola," Jordan said, a hint of laughter behind his words. "I mean, really, Jackson, what the hell are you going to do with a crossbow? Do you want a trench coat and cowboy hat to go with it?"

Jordan's and Jackson's laughter was a bit more prominent from the speaker on the walkie-talkie.

"Not everyone is a weapons specialist and marksman,

Jordan. I brought a slingshot for you just in case," Jackson said as he continued to laugh.

A small, yet crooked smile made its way through all the tension I was carrying as I laughed at the banter between Jackson and Jordan. Those two had become pretty good friends through the years, and laughter was usually a part of their interactions. I appreciated Jordan for being such a positive influence in Jackson's life. Looks like I picked the wrong guy.

"Alright, guys, enough with the jokes. Do any of you see anything unusual?" I asked.

"This is Bourbon Street on Mardi Gras night. Everything out here is unusual. Crowds of people gathered together, showing their naughty parts for fun. I can count at least six gathered groups with cell phone cameras being held in the air and someone in the center of that group showing some flesh," Jackson said. His sigh was apparent over the airwaves. "I can count four groups gathered around as many women with pretty large titt—I mean, breasts with a ton of beads around their necks," Jackson continued.

I stared at the walkie-talkie and shook my head at Jackson's comments. "Nice catch there, Jackson. Remember, I'm not one of the boys," I said. My tone was firm.

"10-4, Auntie. Just keeping you updated. Nothing unusual. Well, unless you count the largest crowd gathering of mostly women surrounding a guy who I think just took off all of his clothes. Wait . . . shit! It's him. He's on my block. I'm headed down." Jackson's panicked voice abruptly ended.

I jumped over the ledge of the rooftop onto the fire escape staircase immediately below. Maneuvering down the metal stairs, into the moistened alleyway, an eruption of screams came from the street. The familiar sight of scores of people running chaotically in the streets mirrored the events of this morning. The crowd parted swiftly as if they were allowing me the view I needed. Some fell to the ground, while others tripped over the people at their feet.

Frank stood in his beastly form in the middle of Bourbon Street with a freshly bitten victim at his feet, bleeding from his side. I pulled Corbin from its holster and aimed for Frank's head. He moved as I fired. The bullet penetrated the wall of the nearby building as the beast lunged and grabbed another victim, sinking his teeth into her. The color red bled onto the green and gold stripes of her form-fitting pants. His speed was overwhelming as I tried to take aim again. I couldn't keep up with his uncanny agility.

He ripped through the crowd of victims, tearing away at their flesh bite after bite. His razor-sharp claws sliced through the limbs of the people that attempted to flee.

Bodies fell onto the moistened, trash covered pavement as the screams of the injured multiplied. Heart pounding, my hands shook as I ran toward Frank. I was unable to keep pace with the trail of blood-soaked people he left behind.

Jackson and Jordan made their way to the beast from the other end of the street. Jackson with Guardian in his hand and Jordan with his sawed-off, double-barrel shotgun. It was too dangerous to fire Corbin with Jackson and Jordan in my line of sight, not to mention the crowd of people. Frank continued to sink his canines into person after person, half of his torso covered in the blood from his victims.

"STOP!" I screamed.

The creature stilled and turned toward me. Jackson, Jordan, and I surrounded him. Frank's creepy, blood-soaked grin pointed once again in my direction. The squint of his glowing red eyes were a tell of his ill intent toward me.

Desperately, I reached for Corbin as Frank moved toward me. I slipped backward as a massive, dark-colored blur struck Frank from its left side and sent him into the exterior brick wall of the bar next to us. Frank let out a high-pitched growl as his body slammed against the brick. The massive, black furred creature pinned Frank to the wall. Its claws struck Frank repeatedly, tearing away the flesh and fur from his chest. With the points of his claws penetrating his neck, ripping at the abdomen with its other hand, slicing open the flesh of Frank.

"Oh, shit. There's two of them," Jordan said in an unusually calm tone.

The familiar size and strength of the werewolf that attacked Frank left little doubt. I had only seen it twice before. Still, no doubt about what and who it was. I knew it was Charles.

Frank pushed Charles away. His body flew across the narrow street onto the pavement. Frank growled as he attacked Charles, ripping at his chest with his claws. The three of us watched as the two vicious werewolves gnawed at each other. Their mutated bodies clashed against each other and against nearby buildings as they fought, wreaking havoc. Crowds gathered at the spectacle. The beastly blows spattered blood along the street as their claws ripped fur and flesh from their bodies.

"Jordan, you have the shotgun. Aim at Frank's head. If you get a hit, I'll follow with the silver rounds directly into the exposed brain. Jackson, hang back. We don't know how Charles will react. He might not like us interfering," I yelled.

The creatures' erratic movements as they fought made it difficult for any of us to get a clear shot. Jackson, Jordan, and I continued to circle around them as they tore the flesh from one another. The front window of a nearby bar shattered as Frank slammed Charles against it. The red flash of the neon sign that hung above bathed shadows of a blood-red tint in parts of both monsters already covered in blood.

Frank clawed at Charles' face and chest. Blood poured from him. Charles' growls weakened into moans as he stumbled backward. Dozens of onlookers screamed. Frank swung his claws at Charles, tearing his throat open. Blood sprayed the crowd. Charles reached for his throat with his snout pointed up as he gasped for air. His body thumped as it fell to the ground. Charles lay still with his arms stretched out.

The prideful grin on Frank's beastly face exposed his blood soaked gums. Frank turned to the crowd and growled. The sound reverberated down my spine. Jordan stepped toward Frank, shotgun raised and fired. Chucks of fur and flesh splattered against the brick of the building. Jordan's shot exposed the beast's red and ivory skull. Jackson hurried behind him, releasing and thrusting Guardian's blade through the creature's back.

A small portion of the tip of the machete's blade protruded through his belly. Frank moaned in agony as his back hand struck Jordan across the face. His body fell limp to the ground. Frank turned around to face Jackson. The Guardian still protruded through him. I pulled Corbin as Frank's razor-sharp claws wrapped around Jackson's left arm.

Jackson squirmed and pulled to get free. "L—Let go of me!" Jackson yelled.

I squeezed the trigger and fired the five remaining rounds I had into the head of the werewolf. The creature swiftly lifted and dropped his other arm and sliced through Jackson's forearm. Blood squirted from Jackson's severed stump and spilled to the ground. Frank dropped the other portion of Jackson's arm. Jackson's bloodcurdling scream sent sharp pains through my stomach.

"Nooooo!" I screamed. Tears fell from my eyes. I continued to pull the trigger and produced nothing but a rotating barrel and repeated clicks from the hammer as it fell.

Frank's haunting grin pointed in my direction again as he stepped toward me. I froze. I felt as if my legs were encased in cement. Seeing Jackson roll in agony on the filthy street, I glanced over at him. Jordan lay unconscious. A calmness set over me as I watched the creature approach and tower over me. The rotten stench of its hot breath assaulted me.

"I can't wait to taste you," Frank snarled.

I was ready, and I was exhausted. The sight of the beast was intolerable as I closed my eyes and accepted my fate. The night air fell silent. I heard no crowd noise, no music, not even the growl of the beast that stood in front of me. Warm blood spattered across my face. There was no pain.

The unexpected scream of Frank forced me to open my eyes and notice sharp, blackened claws protruding from Frank's neck. Blood again sprayed my face as another set of claws ripped through Frank's throat. As Frank's body bucked and buckled, his desperate, gurgled growls were muffled.

Charles climbed onto Frank's back as he pulled him away from me. I watched in awe as Charles growled and continued to slice through Frank's throat as he pulled his claws apart. The flesh and tendons in Frank's neck reached their limits, then snapped. Frank's screams became quiet as Charles severed his father's head from his body. Frank's lifeless body collapsed to the pavement. Charles stood over it with Frank's head, clutched by the hair, still in his hand. His glowing red eyes stared at me with satisfaction.

I stared at Charles for a few moments, conflicted with the satisfaction of what he did and the sight of the werewolf that had killed my parents. Averting my eyes, I rushed over and kneeled next to Jackson, still screaming in pain. I removed a strap from my shoulder holster and tightened it above Jackson's wound.

Jordan moaned as he came to.

"Looks like I still have both of my guys with me. Laying down on the job as usual," I said, as I exhaled sharply.

I turned at the sound of multiple footsteps as they approached. Several uniformed police officers and emergency medical persons gathered around. The naked, headless human shaped body of Frank lay lifeless in the same spot he fell. Charles was nowhere to be found.

CHAPTER
TWENTY-THREE

"I WANTED BETTER FOR YOU." — NOLA

Thursday—Two days after Mardi Gras

"You know, I can't keep sneaking chocolate to you like this. The nurses will keep me from seeing you," Chloe said. She gently caressed Jackson's shoulder as he gleefully chewed the chocolate and peanut butter combo.

Two days post-surgery after the partial loss of an arm and in a hospital bed and Jackson's biggest concern was nursing a sweet tooth.

"Over my dead body," I said. "As far as I'm concerned, you're family. Jackson needs your support right now. Besides, a little chocolate never hurt anyone."

"Exactly! Besides, I lost a few pounds just a couple of days ago. I can take a few extra calories. Chocolate goes well with painkillers," Jackson said. He quickly bit into another piece of candy. His bright smile and infectious laugh followed as he peered down at his partially missing limb, heavily bandaged and wrapped post-surgery. "How's Jordan, by the way?"

"He's resting at home. He'll be up and about in a day or so. Probably will come by to see you once he's feeling better. Jordan took a pretty hard hit," I said.

Jackson shook his head in agreement as he leaned back a little further in the hospital bed. Chloe clutched Jackson's remaining hand with both of hers. The hospital room fell silent. I reflected on everything Jackson had been through. How similar our paths early on in life had been. The loss of both parents. The trauma we had to endure. The scars.

"Auntie, I see your tears. It's okay. I don't regret anything. It's clearer to me now than before. What we do is important, but it has dangerous and sometimes permanent consequences," Jackson said.

"I wanted better for you," I said.

Jackson smiled at me. He and Chloe glanced at each other and shared a small giggle.

"Maybe I can ease your concern a little. Chloe and I have been talking, and we have some ideas for a prosthetic. A couple of talented engineers, remember?" he said with a smirk, tapping his temple with his finger.

I didn't share their optimism.

"Any luck on the Charles front?" The smile on Jackson's face fell. His facial expressions turned emotionless.

"Nothing. I haven't heard from him, and I haven't had time to look yet. He may have left town if he doesn't know how we feel about things now. It's a lot to process," I answered.

Jackson nodded gently. "I don't like him. In fact, I hate him. But he needs to know I'm grateful to him for saving my life. He saved all of our lives."

A sharp pain rose in the pit of my stomach at the thought of thanking Charles for anything.

I closed my eyes and inhaled deeply. "We'll find him, Jackson," I replied.

The door of the hospital room swung open. The heavy door's rush of air briefly chilled the already cold room, swirling the scents of bleach and rubbing alcohol. The smell was stomach-churning. Dr. Cruz and Nurse Thornton walked in with a sense of urgency.

Dr. Cruz's stride was long as he approached the bedside with silver clipboard in hand. He towered over Jackson as he flipped through the pages of the chart attached to the clipboard. A smile was consistently present as he set the chart down and gently squeezed various parts of Jackson's wounded arm. Rows of his discolored and crooked teeth were visible behind his overgrown and unkempt mustache. Nurse Thornton, much shorter in stature and rivaling the thin build of her co-worker, took Jackson's blood pressure as she rapidly squeezed the black rubber bulb in her hand.

"So, how are we feeling today?" Dr. Cruz asked as he continued to squeeze Jackson's arm.

"Doing good, Doc. Pain meds are kick-ass," Jackson answered. His smile was present once again.

Chloe slapped him on his shoulder just above the blood pressure cup. "Stop playing around."

We all smiled as Chloe kept Jackson on the straight path.

"You have a strong one there, Mr. Williams. I'd hold on to her if I were you," Dr. Cruz said.

"I plan on it," Jackson replied.

The sound of the deflating pressure cup and release of the Velcro re-focused me. "How is he doing, Dr. Cruz?" I asked, rubbing my frigid hands together.

"Surgery went fantastic. Swelling is reduced, and nerve

endings are responsive. There's good blood flow throughout the remainder of the arm. He's in good shape. There's a lot of physical therapy in the future, but Mr. Williams should be good to go home in a day or so."

Hand on my chest, I exhaled sharply in relief.

Jackson and Chloe both smiled after hearing Dr. Cruz's words.

"Thank you, Doctor!" I said.

"Glad I could come through for you," Dr. Cruz said. He smiled nervously as he tapped the pen he was holding in the palm of his other hand.

"Go ahead, Dr. Cruz. Tell them," Nurse Thornton said, eyes wide with insistence.

"Nurse Thornton and I are friends. We hang out a lot, and we love the city." Dr. Cruz tapped the pen in his hand faster. "We were on Bourbon Street on Mardi Gras night. We saw just about everything. It was terrifying. Neither one of us thought we would see anything like that up close."

"We both knew who you were and what you did . . . the stories. I know I didn't quite believe it. Dr. Cruz was always a little more open-minded." Nurse Thornton gave Dr. Cruz a crooked smile and a wink.

"He's especially a fan of the both of you. He even knows both of your weapons of choice by their nam—"

"Corbin and Guardian!" Dr. Cruz shouted. His smile was bigger than before. "I can see Corbin hanging right there by your side, Ms. Maor, but I have to say when I saw Jackson extend Guardian, it was probably the coolest thing I ever saw. That's some damn good ingenuity."

The grin on Jackson's face stretched to its limit.

I rolled my eyes in response. I never expected the doctor to be a fanboy.

"Yeah. He's a big nerd. I love him, though," Nurse Thornton said.

"I'll never live this down, will I?" I turned and asked Jackson.

"No. No, you won't," Jackson laughed.

I shook my head with a smile. This was a well-deserved moment of levity, especially for Jackson. The sight of his smile still filled me.

"I really have to ask . . . " Dr. Cruz said. The smile on his face reflected the glee a young boy would have on Christmas morning.

"Cruz, don't," Nurse Thornton said.

"I have to," Dr. Cruz said with excitement in his eyes as he looked at me. "I saw the handle of the Guardian in the bag with Mr. Williams' other belongings. Can you do it? Extend it, I mean? I have to see it up close."

Jackson nodded his head in affirmation without hesitation, smile still present. Everyone in the room stared at me with anticipation. I glanced over at the clear plastic bag, which sat in a chair in the far corner of the room.

I nodded in agreement. "Okay, I'll do it from over by the chair. No other hands will touch it besides mine. It's too sharp and too dangerous for someone hands that's not used to it," I said as I walked over to the chair and removed the rubber grip of Guardian.

The room fell silent as Dr. Cruz and Nurse Thornton stared wide-eyed with anticipation. Nurse Thornton seemed to be just as excited to see it as Dr. Cruz as she clutched his arm with both hands.

I rolled my thumb over the small button on the grip. "Ready?" I asked.

"Oh, yeah!" Dr. Cruz replied.

I pressed the button, and the machete blade of Guardian extended. The vibrations from the force reverberated up my arm.

"That. Was. Awesome!" Dr. Cruz yelled.

"Cruz! This is a hospital," Nurse Thornton said.

"Oh, yeah. Sorry. This is so unprofessional. Thank you for that."

Everyone laughed at his child-like reaction.

His smile dropped almost as fast as it appeared as he stared at the floor. "As I said, we were out there that night. We know it was a werewolf, and we saw how many people it hurt. Do you know how many people were bitten? Or where the other one that killed it went?" Dr. Cruz asked.

"I tried to get a count of those that went to the hospitals for bites. It wasn't easy with Jackson and Jordan down. A lot of the staff didn't want to part with any patient information. I can't blame them. Just doing their jobs." I put Guardian down across the handles of the chair. Thoughts of that night knotted my stomach. "Best guess with what information we have, there were about fifty or so people injured. At least two-thirds of them were bitten."

Dr. Cruz blinked his eyes rapidly. His face turned pale, almost the color of the sheets on Jackson's bed.

"Fifty possible werewolves now in the city. How? How can you possibly hunt so many before they change and kill others?"

"That's the thing, Dr. Cruz. We can't. People will die. Just like your job, our job doesn't end. We have to stay the course," I said.

The looks on Dr. Cruz and Nurse Thornton's faces were difficult to watch. I'd seen it before. The realization of what was going on in the world. Even when someone thought they knew, the new information they receive put it all together for them. In the worst possible way.

"Nurse Thornton, Mr. Williams is due for his next dose of pain meds. Let's get that to him so he can get some rest." Dr. Cruz's tone was bland, void of any emotion. A stark difference from the man only minutes ago. "I have rounds I need to make. It's been a pleasure meeting you both, and you too, Chloe. I suggest you let Mr. Williams rest."

Both left the room with the same urgency they had arrived with. The cold reality of it all was left behind.

Hours later, the temperature of the darkened hospital room had dropped to what seemed to be a relentless, bitter cold in the absence of any more visitors. Goosebumps covered my exposed skin as I curled up in the fetal position in a chair next to Jackson's bed. The scar on my face throbbed as I stroked it with the back of my hand. Odd thing was it was the only one of my many scars over my body that still hurt occasionally. The feeling of the bumpy scar tissue across my face and the sight of clean white bandages wrapped around the wound from Jackson's severed arm reminded me of everything we'd lost. My parents, his parents, Tammy, Priestess Nadia, James, and so many other good people that had fallen to dark dwellers of evil.

This kid had already given so much. Jackson had become a man that both his father and his mother would be proud of.

Tears dropped from my eyes. I wiped them away as quickly as they fell.

"Don't tell me you're watching some sappy movie on your phone or something? What's with the tears?" Jackson said with a smile. His raspy voice was dry from the sleep and pain meds.

"I'm sitting here thinking about you, you jerk."

Jackson shifted in his bed, attempting to push himself to sit up a little higher. "Where's Chloe? Another chocolate run, I hope."

"Nope. I sent her home to get some rest. The poor girl was exhausted. I needed to give her a break from your bullshit, anyway."

Jackson laughed. "Nice! I see I'm rubbing off on you a bit. Good. You could afford to lighten up a little bit."

All I could do was shake my head at him. The kid had a quick wit.

The door to the room crept open. Its soundless movement wiped the grins off both of our faces. A shadowy figure with a familiar muscular silhouette entered.

The towering frame brought conflicted feelings within me. I furrowed my brow and squinted in the darkened room to get a clearer look at his face. My heart thumped feverishly in my chest as I exhaled sharply. The lump in my throat made it hard to swallow.

"Hi." The voice was timid in its approach.

"Charles? Is that you, Charles?" Jackson asked.

Charles approached the foot of the bed next to me. "It's me, kid. Man, am I happy to see you're okay," Charles said as he turned and looked at me. "Hey, Nola. It feels good to put my eyes on you again, sweetheart. I tried to get in yesterday, but it was a little too active. I didn't want to be seen. I wasn't sure if word was out that I was the other werewolf out there. It was much easier to sneak through tonight."

"Where have you been? We've been waiting for you," I said as I found the brightness of his eyes in the darkened room. I could feel my heartbeat in my ears.

Charles' gaze bounced between me and Jackson. "I wanted you and Jackson to have some time to clear your heads. There was a lot to process over the past week. Especially with you, baby." Charles said, averted his eyes in shame.

I could only look at Jackson as my hands shook and my eyes watered. Jackson raised his brow in return.

"Did you know how to kill Frank all this time?" I asked.

"No. I barely understood what exactly he was... what I am. It was instinct... and rage. He knew I was out here all these years, and he didn't want to be a father to me. He abandoned me and my mother. He killed Tammy, someone I loved like a sister. Then he wanted to kill more of the people I loved. He wanted to take you and Jackson from me. No!" Charles' jawline tensed as he clenched his fist. "Our blood feud was short, but I have the feeling that when my sister finds out what I did, it won't be," Charles said.

"You did what you had to do. He took Tammy from us. You saved Auntie Nola's life. You saved my life. Thank you for that," Jackson said, pounding his fist against his chest lightly.

I placed my hand on Charles' shoulder and kissed him gently on the cheek. "Thank you is right. I would have lost Jackson if it wasn't for you. I owe you."

Charles smiled. He exhaled in relief as my hand gently rubbed his back.

"Chuck, I want you to know I get it now. I don't like that you kept secrets from us, but I can see why you did it. You wanted to be a father figure to me, and I made it difficult. I can also see why you made the mistakes you made because you didn't have a father figure in your life to draw from." Jackson smiled as he stared back at Charles.

As my eyes filled with tears, I turned away to hide them.

"You have no idea what this means to me, Jackson. For you and Nola to forgive—"

Blood splattered against Jackson's hospital gown and portions of his face. Charles' head hitting the hospital floor mimicked the sound of a bouncing ball against the pavement. His body made a louder thump as it collapsed to the floor. Blood squirted from his headless torso with the slowing rhythm of his failing heart like a fountain.

The crimson-colored liquid dripped from Guardian; my hand still tightly clutched around its handle.

"How did it feel?" Jackson asked with a crooked smirk.

"It felt out-fucking-standing. Years of anticipation, frustration, and anger satisfied with the swing of a machete," I replied calmly.

"How did you know he would come?" Jackson asked.

"I knew he believed he loved me. He was lying to himself. He was lying to me. If I were you, Jackson, I wouldn't believe a word he said either. I knew he would show up to try to weasel his way back into our lives." I wiped both sides of Guardians' blade on the side of my pants, retracting the blade back into the handle.

"Are you okay?"

"I'm good. He deserved it. Charles got off easy, if you ask me. He killed your parents, and he was there in Dalyville while that banshee tore through the town. He could have done something then. He didn't," Jackson said.

The door to the room once again swung open, striking Charles' head, causing it to roll a couple of feet back to the body. His eyes were still open. Dr. Cruz gasped as his eyes widened and his mouth hanging open. He shut and locked the door behind himself.

"What in the hell is going on?" Dr. Cruz asked. He trembled, his voice shaky, as he stared at Charles' headless body.

"Well, doc, here's your chance to be part of the team." I stepped around the pool of blood from Charles' corpse and walked a little closer to him. "What you see in front of you is the other werewolf from that night."

Dr. Cruz cut his eyes toward me; his brow curled in confusion. "But why would you—"

"He isn't on our side, Doc," I interrupted. "He helped us that night, but he was still hunting and killing innocents. I wanted to try to kill him while he was in human form. I thought it would be easier. Charles showed us how to do it the night he killed Frank. Silver wasn't working, but decapitation seemed to work for him. I needed to see if it would work for us."

Dr. Cruz nodded.

"Can you keep this between us, Dr. Cruz?" I asked.

"I can do better than that." Dr. Cruz reached into his pocket and pulled out his cell phone. A quick tap of the phone's screen and he was talking with someone on the other end. "Honey, I need you in the room with our guest. Bring a stretcher and plenty of sheets." Dr. Cruz paused as he listened to the voice on the other end. "No, not towels. I want this to look like a medical event. We're going to have to get our hands dirty and clean this up."

"Dr. Cruz coming through," Jackson said with a hint of excitement.

"Doc, I have somewhere I take these things to dispose of the remains. Can we get this outside to my car?" I asked.

"No, but I know an ambulance driver that owes me a favor."

"Can he be trusted?"

"Yes. It's Nurse Thorntons' brother. If you ask me, you need all three of us. Let's get this cleaned up."

EPILOGUE
"OKAY GUYS, I'M IN POSITION." — NOLA

Six months later.

THE BRIGHTNESS of the full moon sat prominently in the night sky. It allowed for a well-lit narrow street in the Tremé neighborhood that would otherwise make someone a little wary to walk down. The cooler fall air made the hunt much more enjoyable after the punishing New Orleans' summer heat. I was pretty sure the entire team would agree with me on that point. The hunt had filled the past few months. Werewolves had terrorized the city and wreaked havoc on the city's nightlife. Even after his death, Frank was able to accomplish a sliver of his twisted plan to make New Orleans his wolf's den. It was only a sliver, and I still had plenty of silver to work with.

"Okay guys, I'm in position," I said as I keyed up the walkie-talkie.

There was a brief pause before the sound of one of the

voices came through on the other end. "I have my eyes on it. It looks like it's standing in the alleyway just around the corner from you," Jordan said. The smooth baritone sound of his voice was still a bit of a distraction.

"Yeah, probably waiting for some poor unsuspecting soul to wander by to have for dinner," Chloe said.

Chloe and Jackson were inseparable and insisted that they always went on any assignment together. Right next to each other, annoyingly so.

"We have three of the four possible routes covered. Odds are we'll get to put this one down as long as it takes the bait," Jackson said.

I rolled my eyes after I heard Jackson's bait comment. "Bait? Is that what I am in this catastrophe of an outfit? Whose plan was this again?"

"You know this was our idea, baby. We all agreed on it. Well, the outfit was my idea," Jordan said with a small laugh.

"I can't believe I agreed to wear this. It's embarrassing. A white halter top, pink tights, a tutu that is way too short, and a pink wig . . . All of my goodies are hanging out. This isn't very tactical."

"We needed an outfit that would stand out. One that would make you look like someone coming from the Quarters that had a little too much fun. These werewolves know that we've killed several of them since their transformation. Everyone recognizes you. With so many still out there, we need to be a little more creative. Time for something a little bit outside the norm. Something that would look a little too delicious to pass up," Jordan said.

"Is that what I look like? Do I look delicious?" I said with a smile as I gently bit down on my lower lip.

"Oh yes. Yes, you do, baby," Jordan answered.

"Yuck! Can we please focus here? Nobody wants to hear all that. Focus. No mistakes or somebody could lose a limb," Jackson said.

Laughter burst from me. It was loud enough to echo throughout the empty late-night air.

That boy is hilarious.

"Heads up, everyone. That laugh caught its attention. It's on the move. Everyone, start making your way to Nola. Keep your distance. We want it to only see her," Jordan said.

The beast made its way to the intersection at the other end of the block. Its six-foot frame stood in the center of the crossroads and peered around, lifting its snout into the air, trying to catch the scent of something it liked. The irony struck me as it stood there trying to make a decision. A life-or-death decision, unbeknownst to it.

The creature fixated on the street that led to Jackson and Chloe. It must have picked up a scent or spotted something it wanted. I shouldn't be worried. Jackson and Chloe could handle themselves. Hell, Jackson was more dangerous than any of us with that new prosthetic he and Chloe designed. Still, I would rather it dealt with me.

"Yooo hooooo! Here, doggy!" I yelled, waving one hand in the air.

Baring teeth, it turned in my direction. It howled toward the night sky after it set its sights on me. I stood fast in the middle of the street. My hand gripped the handle of Corbin, tucked in the tutu against the small of my back. Its claws ripped into the concrete as it raced toward me. I pulled Corbin from behind me and took aim at the werewolf's head. Its teeth drew closer, thirsting to tear into my flesh.

I squeezed the trigger. As the silver round released from Corbin's barrel, thunder echoed in the air. The bullet ripped through the skull of the creature, sending blood and brain matter out the back of it. The werewolf's lifeless body fell and tumbled a few feet closer before coming to a stop. I looked up to see Jackson, Jordan, and Chloe as they ran toward me. When I looked back down at our hunt for the night, I smiled.

"Looks like you ran into the wrong family." I holstered Corbin and pulled down at the still rising tutu. "Damn it. I have to get out of these clothes."

QUIESCENT: BLOOD FEUD

The End.

www.ingramcontent.com/pod-product-compliance
Lightning Source LLC
LaVergne TN
LVHW010320070526
838199LV00065B/5619